EVERYONE L!

PRAISE FOR *THE ANGEL EXPERIMENT*

"**Book of the week**....Pace, action, mystery, and cool." —*London Times*

"Like the best sort of video game or action movie, in book form. It **shows the promise of becoming a favorite.**" —*Cleveland Plain Dealer*

"**Speed, suspense, excitement.** . . . Nonstop action carries this pageturner breathlesly from start to finish." —*Kirkus Reviews*

"The claim of '**addictive**' is completely true. . . . The writing is quick, fresh, funny, [and] smart." —*Toronto Sun*

"A never-ending series of twists and action. . . . A fantastic romp that's **hard to put down.**" —*Virginian-Pilot*

PRAISE FOR *SCHOOL'S OUT—FOREVER*

"**Five stars!** An action-packed, thrilling, and truly amazing book." —BookReporter.com

"Readers are in for **another exciting wild ride**...leaving [them] breathless for the follow-up." —*Kirkus Reviews*

"Patterson's **super-fast pace** keeps the action moving and the suspense tense." —*Star Ledger* (NJ)

PRAISE FOR *MAX*

"Filled with humor.... Patterson has brought Max and flock into a new direction and given them wings.... This group of kids is going to be having **one massive fun ride** well into the future."
—EdgeBoston.com

"This is the best one yet." —BestsellersWorld.com

"Will leave fans anxious for more of Max's adventures."
—Bookloons.com

"This book **will please all Fang lovers immensely.** For all the girls who have been dreaming about Mr. Tall, Dark, and Winged, your prayers have been answered." —not-so-cg.blogspot.com

PRAISE FOR *FANG*

"Mr. Patterson has created **another thrilling adventure** that is sure to capture readers' imaginations.... [His] quick-paced tale of adventure, betrayal, and redemption is full of **vibrant and memorable characters.** It **truly has bite."** —*School Library Journal*

"This **will excite the legions of fans** waiting for this installment in the flock's story." —*Booklist*

"[B]reath-taking.... Maximum Ride fans will not be disappointed in *Fang.* **The high-flying plot and new twists leave the reader begging for more** of Max and the flock." —*Burlington Times-News*

PRAISE FOR *ANGEL*

"Even reluctant readers won't be able to put down this **intense thriller."**
—Barnes & Noble

"A strong installment in the series.... **Fantastic flying descriptions ... will make readers wish they had wings."** —The Associated Press

BOOKS BY JAMES PATTERSON
for Readers of All Ages

THE WITCH & WIZARD NOVELS
Witch & Wizard (with Gabrielle Charbonnet)
The Gift (with Ned Rust)
The Fire (with Jill Dembowski)

THE MAXIMUM RIDE NOVELS
The Angel Experiment
School's Out — Forever
Saving the World and Other Extreme Sports
The Final Warning
MAX
FANG
ANGEL

THE DANIEL X NOVELS
The Dangerous Days of Daniel X (with Michael Ledwidge)
Watch the Skies (with Ned Rust)
Demons and Druids (with Adam Sadler)
Game Over (with Ned Rust)

THE MIDDLE SCHOOL NOVELS
Middle School, The Worst Years of My Life
(with Chris Tebbetts, illustrated by Laura Park)
Middle School: Get Me out of Here!
(with Chris Tebbetts, illustrated by Laura Park)

OTHER ILLUSTRATED NOVELS
Daniel X: Alien Hunter (graphic novel; with Leopoldo Gout)
Daniel X: The Manga, Vol. 1–2 (with SeungHui Kye)
Maximum Ride: The Manga, Vol. 1–5 (with NaRae Lee)
Witch & Wizard: The Manga, Vol. 1 (with Svetlana Chmakova)

*For previews of upcoming books in these series and other information, visit
www.MaximumRide.com, www.Daniel-X.com, www.WitchAndWizard.com,
and www.MiddleSchoolBook.com.*

For more information about the author, visit www.JamesPatterson.com.

FANG

A MAXIMUM RIDE NOVEL
JAMES PATTERSON

LITTLE, BROWN AND COMPANY
New York   Boston

Copyright © 2010 by James Patterson

Little, Brown and Company
Hachette Book Group
1290 Avenue of the Americas, New York, NY 10104
Visit our website at www.lb-teens.com

Little, Brown and Company is a division of Hachette Book Group, Inc.
The Little, Brown name and logo are trademarks of Hachette Book Group, Inc.

The publisher is not responsible for websites (or their content) that are not owned by the publisher.

First Paperback Edition: January 2011
First published in hardcover in March 2010 by Little, Brown and Company

Library of Congress Cataloging-in-Publication Data

Patterson, James
    Fang : a Maximum Ride novel / James Patterson. — 1st ed.
        p. cm.
    Summary: When Max and the Flock discover an unscrupulous scientist who is experimenting on humans in an effort to "improve" the human race, they decide that they must try to stop him, in spite of Angel's prediction about Fang dying.
    ISBN 978-0-316-03619-1 (hc) / ISBN 978-0-316-03831-7 (pb)
    [1. Genetic engineering—Fiction.   2. Adventure and adventurers—Fiction.   3. Science fiction.]   I. Title.
    PZ7.P27653Fan 2010
    [Fic]—dc22   2009044767

10 9 8 7 6 5

RRD-C

Printed in the United States of America

Many thanks to Gabrielle Charbonnet,
my conspirator, who flies high and cracks wise.

To the reader

THE IDEA FOR the Maximum Ride series comes from earlier books of mine called *When the Wind Blows* and *The Lake House,* which also feature a character named Max who escapes from a quite despicable School. Most of the similarities end there. Max and the other kids in the Maximum Ride books are not the same Max and kids featured in those two books. Nor do Frannie and Kit play any part in the series. I hope you enjoy the ride anyway.

"Thank God men cannot fly, and lay waste the sky as well as the earth."

—Henry David Thoreau

BOOK
ONE
MEETING DOCTOR GOD

1

I'M A GIRL OF EXTREMES. When I love something, I'm like a puppy dog (without all the licking). When I'm cranky, I'm a wasp (like, a whole hive of 'em). And when I'm angry, I'm a mother bear with a predator after her cubs: dangerous.

I say this because lately my life seemed to be all about extremes. Like right now, for instance. I was soaring twenty thousand feet in the air with the five people I loved most in the world—and no, we weren't on a plane, hang-gliding, or hot air ballooning. We preferred to use good old-fashioned *wings*. The technology's been around for eons.

If you've ever dreamed you could fly, I can confirm that it's all that and better. Even if you're desperately flying through a subway tunnel to save your life, it's still off the charts. But today, flying over Africa...it was as good as it ever gets. Maybe the best part was that for the first time in a dog's age, we weren't on the run from madmen. We were on a mission—to do good.

"Max!" Iggy called over to me. "Why did they name themselves *Chad*? I mean, *Chad*. It's like naming a whole country Biff or Trey. I don't get it."

"Ig, don't be ignorant," I scoffed. "It's not like all the people there named themselves."

"Why not? *We* named ourselves," Nudge noted, as if I needed to be reminded that we were raised in a lab under the supervision of science geeks.

"Only 'cause we're special." I gestured to her twelve-foot wingspan. "Hey, check that out!" I pointed to a Martian-like rock formation in the distance.

Fang turned his head and gave me one of his classic half smiles—you know, like the kind of smile Mona Lisa would have had if she were a guy. A teenage guy with long-ish scruffy hair, dark eyes, and a leather jacket. Mmmmm.

The whole trip had been as exhilarating as one of Fang's killer smiles. Even the hundreds of miles of shifting, mysterious desert dunes had been amazing. We're world travelers and all—we've lived in wilds as extreme as Death Valley and Antarctica—but there was something downright otherworldly about what I'd seen below as we crossed over—oh, crap, I'd forgotten the names of all of the different countries.

"Mauritania, Algeria, Mali, Niger, and Chad together

are about sixty-eight percent desert," Angel recited, reading my mind. Literally. She's powerful like that.

"Whatever. It's too much freaking desert," Angel's brother, Gazzy, complained. "I wouldn't mind seeing a few cows chomping away on some grass right about now."

"A-plus-plus on the geography quiz, Angel. Gazzy, Iggy, extra credit when you check your attitudes at the door." Even without parents, somehow I'd picked up the language. Seems to work when you're the leader. "Listen, I know some of you are a little cranky from the long flight, but this is our chance to finally *help people. Real* people," I emphasized, as if we'd grown up in a plastic bubble or something. Well, we kind of *had.* Do dog crates in labs count?

"Real people," Fang clarified. "As in, not just a bunch of wack-job scientists."

"Yup. Did it ever occur to you guys," I continued grandly, "that when we were told we had to save the world, it might have actually meant saving people—like, one at a time? Sending a message around the world about people in need is great and all, but actually feeding people, giving people medical help and stuff? We've never done that before. I mean, this could be it, guys. Our destiny."

"Max is right," Angel agreed, in a very un-Angel-like manner. We didn't see eye-to-eye on much these days.

"Word on the street is that *you* have to save the world, Max," Iggy reminded me. "The rest of us? Not so much."

Twit. Always trying to take the easy way out.

Not Fang, though. "Hey, Max, wherever you go to save the world—I will follow..." He did the killer half-smile thing. "Mother Teresa."

My stomach flip-flopped as if I'd folded my wings and plunged into free fall. *Hello, Max the Puppy.*

I had exactly five seconds to enjoy sainthood before I caught sight of three black dots in the distance—and they appeared to be moving straight toward us.

Looked like Mama Bear's cubs were in danger. And you know what that meant:

Bye-bye, Saint Max. Time to be a hellion again.

2

"INCOMING!" I SHOUTED to my flock. "Down, down, *down!*"

Fast-moving objects directed at the flock usually belong to one of three categories: bullets, mutant beings with a taste for bird kid, or vehicles hired by an evil megalomaniac wanting to kidnap us and use our powers. Which might explain why I was working on the assumption that the three black dots meant one thing and one thing only: imminent death.

"Max! *Relax!*" Fang managed to stop me before I could execute my dive. "I think those are the CSM cargo planes."

It was the Coalition to Stop the Madness (CSM), the

activist group my nonwinged mom was involved with, that had asked us to go on this humanitarian relief mission to Chad and to help publicize the work they were doing there. And what with our previous adventures helping them combat global warming and ocean pollution, we were slowly being turned from feral, scavenging outlaws on the lam into Robin Hoody do-gooders. Meanwhile, I was still supposed to save the world at some point. My calendar was full, full, full.

So full that I'd forgotten this was the part of the journey where we were supposed to meet up with the CSM planes so we could be guided into the refugee camp.

I gave Fang a thank-you-for-saving-me-from-myself look. When his eyes met mine, I shivered down to my sneakered toes.

Gazzy called over to me, "I can't see anything!"

"I can't see anything either!" Iggy complained.

"I'm rolling my eyes, Ig." I had to tell him that because he couldn't see me do it, what with his blindness and all.

"No, there's, like, dust clouds below," Gazzy clarified.

I glanced down, and sure enough—the blurry endlessness of sand was even more blurry.

"Not dust devils," Fang said. His dark feathers were covered with a layer of dust, and grit was caked around his eyes and mouth.

"No." I peered downward again.

Just then Angel said, "Uh-oh," which is always enough

to make my blood run cold. In the next second, I focused sharply on a few dark specks at the front of the dust clouds. One of the dark specks raised a tiny dark toothpick.

This time I knew for sure that I wasn't overreacting.

"Guns!" I shouted. "They've got guns!"

3

"QUICK! UP!" FANG SHOUTED, just as the first bullets strafed the air around me with ominous hisses.

I angled myself upward, only to see the shiny silver underbelly of one of the CSM planes, now flying right above us. It was pressing downward—the rough landing strip was maybe a quarter mile away.

"Drop back!" I yelled. We all went vertical as the planes continued to come down practically on our heads. To escape from the bullets, we'd had to fly up right under them. The engines were way too close—the noise was deafening.

"Watch it!" I yelled, as one plane's landing gear almost hit Iggy. "Drop down! Drop down!" Bullets are bad, but getting smushed by landing gear, toasted by jet engine exhaust, or sucked into the front of an engine were all much less fixable.

I could now make out the sun-browned faces of the men on...oh, geez, were those *camels*? The men continued to aim their rifles at us, and I felt a bullet actually whiz by my hair. In about half a second, my brain processed the following thoughts lightning fast:

1) A bullet hitting the fuel tank on a plane: not a good situation.
2) Slowing down not good: slow + bird kids = drop like rocks.
3) Speeding up not good: fast bird kids + faster planes = getting flattened.
4) The only choice was to go on the offensive.

Fortunately, I'm very comfortable with being offensive—at least on the not-infrequent occasions when someone's trying to gun down my flock.

"Dive!" I shouted. "Knock 'em down!"

I tucked my wings flat against my back and began to race groundward like a rocket. At this speed, these shooters would need radar and a heat tracer to land a bullet on me. I could actually see the whites of their eyes now, which were widening in surprise.

"*Hai-yah!*" I screamed—just for fun, really—as I swung my feet down and came to a screeching halt by smashing my heels right into a rider's back. He flew off the camel, rifle pinwheeling through the air, and felt the joy of being airborne himself for about three seconds before he landed right in front of his pal's camel.

"Get the rest!" I ordered the flock. "Free the beasts!"

There were about ten of these armed riders—no match for six hot, angry bird kids. We were used to dodging bullets; these guys were not used to aiming at fast-moving flying mutants. And the bonuses of being aloft are infinite: Snatching a rifle from the grip of a maniacal shooter isn't as hard as you might think when you're coming from above and behind.

Iggy flew in sideways and smacked one guy right off his camel, and Gazzy folded his wings around another's face, causing him to panic and fall. I grabbed a gun and used it like a baseball bat, neatly clipping one guy in the gut, knocking him right off his ride. Unfortunately, I didn't rise in time.

Which meant that for the first time in bird kid history, I got plowed into by a panicky galloping camel—with no sense of humor. Its head hit me in the stomach, and I flipped over its neck, landing hard on the saddle.

"Awesome move, Max!" I heard Nudge call from somewhere behind me. Wasn't she busy helping to take these guys out?

My Indiana Jones moment lasted about a second before I was lurched off the beast. Just as my feet hit the sand, I managed to grab a rein and hang on for dear life.

My wings were useless—there was no room to stretch

them out—and my ankles were literally sanded raw before I was able to pull myself up hand over hand and eventually clamber back onto the saddle.

"Whoa, Nelly!" I croaked, gagging on dust. I gripped the saddle with my knees and pulled back on the reins.

This camel did not speak English, apparently. It stretched its neck and ran faster.

"Up and away, Max!" Fang yelled.

I dropped the reins, popped to my feet on top the saddle, and jumped hard, snapping out my wings. And just like that, I became lighter than air, stronger than steel…and faster than a speeding camel.

I watched it race off, terrified, toward the nearest village. Someone was about to inherit a traumatized camel.

This mission was off to a good start.

4

"OKAY, FLOCK," I SAID, finishing wrapping up my bleeding ankles. "So who's ready to start saving the world, one person at a time? Say aye!"

"Aye!" Nudge cheered and took a last swig of water. Just twenty minutes earlier we'd landed in front of the astonished locals. The others, still worn out from the camel crusade, chimed in a little more sluggishly. Except Fang, who gave me a strong and silent thumbs-up.

Patrick Rooney III, our CSM contact, led us to our assigned area. I hadn't seen a refugee camp before. It was basically acres and acres of tattered tents and mud huts. Two larger tents were being set up for donated medical supplies and food. Nudge and Iggy were set to unpacking crates and sorting materials,

Fang to helping set up medical exam stations, which were basically plastic crates with curtains around them.

Gazzy and Angel were, essentially, the entertainment— their pale blond hair and blue eyes were causing a commotion among the refugee kids. Not to mention the wings. Some of the youngest kids were running around, their arms outstretched and flapping, their smiles huge with delight.

Not that there was much to be delighted about. The six of us, the flock, had seen some hard times. We'd eaten out of Dumpsters and trapped small mammals for dinner. I'd eaten my share of rat-b-cue. But these people had nothing. I mean, *really* nothing. Most were skinnier than us lean-'n'-mean bird kids.

"People are going to be coming through here, getting vaccinated against hep B, tetanus, mumps, whatever," the nurse, a guy named Roger, explained. "The grown-ups may be suspicious and unsure; a lot of the kids will be crying."

Okay. I could handle that. I knew being Mother Teresa wasn't gonna be easy.

"Here are some sacks of rice—they weigh sixty pounds each, so get someone to help you move them." That wouldn't be necessary—one of the few advantages to being genetically engineered in a lab. "The adults each get two cups of raw rice." He handed me a measuring cup. "Give the kids these fruit roll-ups. They've never seen them before, so you might have to explain that they're food. Do you speak French?"

"Nooo." Just another one of those pesky gaps in my education. "I don't speak African either."

Roger smiled. "There are thousands of dialects in Africa—Chad alone has two hundred distinct linguistic groups. But Arabic and French are the official languages of Chad—France used to own Chad."

I frowned. "Own it? They're not even *connected*."

"The way England used to own America," Roger explained.

"Oh." I felt really dumb, which is not a common feeling for me, I assure you.

A few minutes later, Fang was by my side, and we were handing out two cups of raw rice per person. It was all I could do not to just give them everything I could get my hands on. Fang and I kept meeting eyes.

"It reminds me of—so long ago—before Jeb sprung us out of the dog crates..." My throat caught, and Fang nodded. He knew it was a painful memory.

But it wasn't the memory that was getting me. It was seeing so many people looking like...like they were still waiting to be let out of their dog crates. Despite everything we'd been through—some of it the stuff of nightmares—we were still way better off than the people here.

I was a little dazed by the time Angel strode up to us, leading a small girl by the hand.

"Hi," said Angel, her face still caked with dust and grit. Her blond curly hair stood out around her head like a halo—which was a bit misleading in her case. "This is Jeanne. Jeanne, this is Max and Fang."

Angel had that look that made me brace myself and prepare to explain that we could *not* adopt this sweet little girl. We'd already adopted two dogs (Total and Akila, now back in the States with my mom, Dr. Valencia Martinez, in Arizona). But this Jeanne was so adorable, I was almost afraid I'd just say what the hey.

Jeanne smiled. "Merci pour tout les aides."

"Uh, okay," I said. Jeanne came and gave me a hug, her thin arms wrapping around me. She patted my shoulder, her small hand rough against the back of my neck. Then she hugged Angel the same way.

"Jeanne has gifts," Angel said seriously. "Kind of like us. She's very special. Let's show Max, Jeanne."

Jeanne smiled shyly and held out her hand, palm up, as if she were waiting for us to put something in it. *Another hungry child, desperate for food.*

Angel pulled an arrowhead-shaped rock from the pocket of her cargo shorts. It was so sharp it looked like the tip of a spear.

"Angel, what the—?"

"Just watch, Max," she said, as she started to drag the rock's point across the heel of Jeanne's open hand.

And blood began to flow.

5

"STOP!" I SCREAMED. Lightning fast, I swept the sharp rock right out of Angel's grasp, and it went spinning off into the dust. "Have you completely lost your mind, Angel?"

"It's okay, Max," Angel assured me, and Jeanne nodded. "Oui, oui."

I dropped to my knees and examined Jeanne's hand while she sucked a finger on her other. She had a thin puncture at least an inch long. "Wait here. I'm gonna run to get a first aid kit," I said breathlessly.

Jeanne grabbed my arm with her nonbloody hand. "Non, non," she said. "Voici." She pointed to her oozing wound.

"I know, I know. I'm so sorry, Jeanne!" I babbled. "Please

forgive Angel. She's a little...unbalanced. I'll fix you up right now. You'll be fine, I promise."

"Yes, she will," Angel said calmly. How badly was I going to kick her butt later?

Jeanne placed the finger she'd been sucking on at one end of the incision and started pressing it.

"Jeepers, don't touch that!" I said. "We need to keep the wound clean—keep it from getting infected." I looked around. "Someone here who speaks French! Tell her not to—"

I broke off as I witnessed something unlike anything I'd seen before. And I'd seen a lot of weird stuff—including brains-on-a-stick (check out book three if you're curious). Most of the weird stuff I'd seen had been nightmarish. But this was...something beautiful. Breathtaking. Miraculous.

As Jeanne ran her finger slowly along the bloody slash, pressing as she went, it closed up right before my eyes.

She had healed herself.

6

"ALL RIGHT, any second now..." The words were clipped, his accent thick. Mr. Chu leaned over his assistant's shoulder, impatiently looking at a blank computer screen. And then, right on time, the screen flickered and split to show two charts, side by side. Points started blinking faintly, and small words began running along different lines: heart rate, temperature, blood oxygen saturation level, and so on.

His assistant peered at the charts for a moment, then typed "Maximum" on one side and "Angel" on the other. Mr. Chu became lost in reviewing the biological data streaming in from the microscopic monitors.

"Mr. Chu? You have a visitor, sir." Another assistant stood in the trailer doorway, one hand on his weapon, as required.

Mr. Chu went down the short, narrow hall to the small receiving room. A young girl in a yellow dress stood there, twisting one of her thin braids between nervous fingers.

"Hello, Jeanne," said Mr. Chu, smiling. Jeanne managed a tiny smile back. "You were successful in your mission," said Mr. Chu, motioning to an assistant.

"Les filles oiseaux sont trés belles," Jeanne said sweetly.

"Here is your reward," said Mr. Chu, taking a lollipop from his assistant and giving it to Jeanne. Her eyes widened, and she eagerly ripped the wrapper off and stuck the candy in her mouth. Her eyes closed in rapture.

Mr. Chu nodded again, and his assistant quickly swabbed Jeanne's upper arm with an alcohol wipe. The whole length of her arm was lined with dots, marking the sites of hundreds of needle insertions. And here was a new one, as the assistant injected the contents of a hypodermic needle into Jeanne's almost nonexistent muscle. It was the first of a dozen injections to come in the next twenty-four hours.

Jeanne had learned to put up with all of the drugs — the pills, the drips, the shots. Without them, the side effects of being a self-healer were much, much worse. The treatments were a small price to pay for such rewards, after all.

Jeanne's closed eyelids flickered a tiny bit as the needle went in, but she swirled the lollipop in her mouth and didn't say a word.

7

WE WORKED ALL DAY, until dusk. The flock is usually chock-full o' stamina, but it kind of depends on getting three or four thousand calories a day. By six o'clock, we were running on empty.

"Max?" said Patrick, walking up to me with a lumpy sack in tow. "Here's some bedding—it's not much, I'm afraid. There's a tent set aside for you guys. Do you want to get it organized before dinner? You have about ten minutes."

"Sure. By the way, Patrick, who was the camel platoon?" I asked.

"Don't know for sure," he said. "But some of the locals have a thing against Americans. It's complicated politics we can talk about later. Right now, if you want to set up..."

"Sure, thanks," I said, taking the sack. I looked at my

tired flock. "You guys wait here — I think chow's coming. And drink some water."

"I'll help you with that," said Fang, nodding at the tent.

"Sure," I said casually, but my heart was already speeding up.

We ducked through the worn nylon flap of our tent, and I dropped the sack. In the next moment we had our arms around each other, ignoring the dust on each other's lips and our hot and sticky skin.

"The flying was amazing, but...I've missed you," Fang murmured, his hands getting stuck in the snarls in my hair.

"Yeah. And this is probably our only chance to be alone for a while."

"I couldn't stand seeing you get shot at today," Fang said, kissing my neck.

I drew back in surprise. "You've seen me get shot at, like, a million times!"

He shrugged, scratching my back between my wings, making me shiver. "It's worse now."

"Yeah, I know what you mean," I said, and held his face so I could kiss him again. It felt like we were in a time-free bubble, the only two people around, and in the ninety-eight-degree weather, I felt like I was burning up from my head to my toes.

"Max! Fang! Dinner!"

I jumped and pulled back. But no one came into the tent, so Fang's lingering hands stroked up and down my arms as we tried to get normal expressions back on our faces. Part of me wanted to stay in there forever and forget the rest of the world, but I immediately felt guilty, thinking of the flock waiting for us outside. I was still responsible for them; we were still a family.

And always would be.

8

"PASS THE . . . GRUB," said Iggy a few minutes later, holding out his hand.

"The brown grub or the yellow grub?" I asked. My face still felt flushed from my time with Fang. I hoped the others couldn't tell.

"Either." Iggy ran a hand through his reddish-blond hair, making it stand up stiffly with dirt and sweat. Later I was going to march everyone to the one water pump in this tent village, pump up a couple gallons of water, and try to decrust the flock as much as possible. We've got certain standards. They're way low, but we have them.

"You guys did great today," said Patrick. "You must be exhausted."

"Um-hm," I mumbled, picking up a white ball of millet paste. Dipped in the peanut–goat stew sauce, it was about a three on the Max Culinary Scale—above roasted desert rat or lizard-on-a-stick, but well below, say, a steak.

Roger, the nurse, handed Iggy a small dented bowl. "Dried fish, mixed with...stuff. Try it."

We ate everything we could get our hands on. Living on the streets had beaten any pickiness out of us. Plus, we burn calories like a race car burns fuel, and we just couldn't afford to not eat—whatever it was.

The fire leaped in front of us, looking pretty and feeling cozy and warm but smelling to high heaven, since its fuel was camel poop. Yes. I mean, a regular *camel* is no bed of roses, but its poop? On fire? The only one not wrinkling his nose was Gazzy. But as soon as the blazing sun had set, the desert temperature had dropped about thirty degrees, and the fire was welcome.

I ate, trying not to miss chocolate, and felt the warmth of Fang's leg pressed against mine, here in the shadows. I was on my third pass of reliving our stolen minutes in the tent and already wondering when we could be alone again. These days I spent a ridiculous amount of time dreaming about someday just being able to spend all day with Fang. Alone.

Now my face was really burning. In my dream, the flock was safe somewhere, Total and Akila weren't there, and no one was chasing us. I would have no worries, no need to be on alert. I could just relax. Which, okay, I suck at, but I was hoping that with practice…

"You guys met Jeanne today, didn't you?" Patrick asked. "The little girl in the yellow dress?"

"She's really special," Angel said solemnly.

"Yes." Patrick shook his head. "She used to have a father and four brothers. They've all died in the past two years, from either HIV or hunger or the outbreaks of civil war that keep happening. Now it's just Jeanne and her mother, and her mom has been diagnosed with HIV."

"Oh, no," Nudge said, tears welling in her eyes. "So she'll be an orphan?"

Patrick nodded sadly. "Most likely. In many other countries people can sometimes live long lives with HIV medications. But it's different here. And there are so many other children like her."

I choked down another millet ball (*Note to self:* Do not bother getting recipe) and looked around at my beloved flock, safe in a circle around the fire. Iggy was staring straight into the flames, able to because he was blind. Gazzy was examining each and every last bowl for any morsel that might have been missed. Nudge had her chin in her hands, looking at the ground, and I knew she was bumming about all the misery here. My life would have been incomplete without each and every one of them.

I glanced into Fang's eyes to find him watching me with dark intensity, and my cheeks flushed again. Could we sneak off, like, into the dark shadows of the desert? Just for a minute?

"Nothing can last forever, Max." It was Angel, eerily interrupting my thoughts. She was scratching at the dirt with a small animal bone. "And actually—I hate to tell you this, but Fang will be the first to die. And it will be soon."

9

FIVE BIRD KID HEADS swiveled toward Angel. Nudge's mouth had dropped open, and Gazzy's eyes were big. Iggy's boyish face creased into wrinkles. My dark, mysterious Fang hardly registered his surprise, as if Angel had just said it was about to rain.

As for me, I felt like Angel had kicked me in the gut.

"What *exactly* do you mean by that?" I finally choked out.

"I'm just saying, Max," said Angel, still playing with her bone. "You always want everything to stay the same. But it can't. We're all getting older. You have a mom. You and Fang are all googly eyed at each other. Nothing stays the same. We can't last forever. And I happen to know that

Fang is going to be the first to die. You're gonna have to learn to live without him. I'm sorry."

My eyes narrowed and I stood up. "How do you know that?" I asked tightly. "What makes you say that?" The rest of the flock was watching, wide-eyed. Only Fang didn't look upset.

"It's okay, Max," he said, patting my leg. "Don't worry about it."

Angel looked at him sadly and shook her head, and something in me broke loose. I grabbed her shirt and pulled her to her feet. Her mouth opened in surprise.

"What. Do. You. Mean," I snarled.

Fang jumped up and tried to pry my hands loose. Nudge tried to get between us. I ignored them, focusing on Angel's face.

"You tell me what you meant," I said, "or I'm gonna..." I had to think of something almost as bad as killing her but not quite. "I'll—I'll cut off all that floofy blond hair of yours while you sleep!"

"Max!" hissed Fang, pulling at me. "Stop it!" But I was still shaking Angel.

"Max, stop," pleaded Nudge, sounding close to tears.

"Is everything okay?" Patrick's concerned voice started to filter into my brain as I realized what I was doing. I'd never almost hurt a member of the flock before. Abruptly, I let go of Angel's shirt. Her face was white.

"Max, gosh," said Nudge, putting her hand on Angel's shoulder.

I was breathing hard, and Fang pushed me back gently, moving me away from Angel. How could she say something like *that* and not explain it?

"Max, come on," said Fang.

I opened my mouth, but then noticed that two people were approaching our fire. This would have to wait.

10

"HELLO," PATRICK SAID as the people got nearer. As they got close, we could see that there was a tall man and a tall kid. They were only silhouettes until they were almost on top of the fire.

"Hello, good evening." The man had a foreign accent and was ridiculously dapper in a crisp, clean seersucker suit.

"Can I help you?" asked Patrick.

"Ah, yes," he said. "I am Dr. Hans Gunther-Hagen. One of my companies is conducting research here—I donated the supply of vaccines your group is using."

Patrick stood and quickly wiped his hands on his shorts before holding one out to Dr. Gunther-Hagen. "Oh, thank you so much!" he said, beaming. "I can't tell you what a difference it makes! We really appreciate your generosity."

The doctor smiled at him. "It was my pleasure. It's a blessing to be able to share my prosperity with others."

Roger leaned over to whisper in my ear. "Huge billionaire. Owns a hundred companies, most in pharmaceuticals."

Another huge billionaire, eh? I wondered if he knew Nino Pierpont, the richest guy in the world, who sometimes funded our little adventures. Like, did billionaires hang out with each other? Talk about the countries they want to buy, that kind of thing?

"I heard that you have the bird children here," he said.

My eyebrows went up. Patrick looked nonplussed and deliberately didn't glance at us.

"Oh?" he managed.

"Yes," the doctor said, sounding friendly and curious. "I'm most interested to meet them. They've gotten such tremendous publicity. I was hoping to ask the leader of the bird children to come have breakfast with me tomorrow morning in my tent."

Seconds ticked by. Patrick and Roger said nothing.

I rose and stepped forward, saying, "That would be me."

At the exact same time, Angel stood, saying, "Sure."

My jaw clenched. On top of everything else, she was now starting one of her campaigns to lead the flock? *Your timing sucks,* I thought at her, and she flicked her eyes at me.

"Ah, fine," said Dr. Gunther-Hagen, rubbing his hands together excitedly. "Splendid! Both of you come, then. But first, I'd like to introduce my...protégé. This is Dylan." He gestured, and the tall kid stepped into the fire's circle of light.

I blinked, wondering what teen heartthrob magazine Dr. Häagen-Dazs had swiped Dylan from. He was as tall as Fang and Iggy, meaning over six feet. His thick, dark-blond hair was shoved carelessly back from a tanned fore-head. Expressive turquoise eyes looked at us with guarded curiosity. He was wearing worn jeans and scuffed, dusty boots. A beat-up suede jacket mostly covered his clean white T-shirt. He was ready for a photo shoot—like, for the top twenty-five hottest guys under the age of twenty.

Of course, Fang would also qualify.

"Hey," I said raspily and nodded, but I couldn't think of anything else to say. And for some reason, that actually bothered me.

"I was particularly hoping *you* could meet Dylan," said the doctor. "He's been putting up with my company, and I'm sure he would benefit from meeting young people like himself."

I rolled my eyes mentally, thinking that of course we were in no way like Dylan.

"Show them, Dylan," said the doctor.

Dylan looked self-conscious but slowly took off his jacket to reveal broad shoulders and muscled arms. He was heavier than Fang, bulkier—maybe he was older? Had more regular access to food?

I was thinking, *Wha*—? when Dylan sort of shrugged his shoulders and *extended his wings*. All fifteen feet of them.

11

I AM NOTHING if not resilient, but usually I can handle only about one humongous life-shaking situation per hour. Now here it was, the second earth-shattering thing in five minutes. That, on top of the millet balls, made for a dangerously unsettled stomach.

"Where'd you come from, Dylan?" Fang's steady and calm voice gave nothing away. He sat down and picked up a small bag of water to drink.

Dylan gave kind of a wry little smile. "A test tube," he said. "A lab."

Dr. Hunker-Gunther smiled and clapped his hands. "Oh, you have so much to talk about! But it is late and we are all tired." He gave an old-fashioned bow. "We will be looking forward to seeing you tomorrow."

We were silent for several moments after they left. My eyes followed their outlines until tents got in the way.

"Well!" said Patrick finally. "I certainly never expected that! Did you know there were more of you?"

"Nope," I said.

I glanced around at the dazed flock, wanting to get Angel alone so I could grill her for more details of her pronouncement about Fang. It would be best not to upset the others by bringing it up again publicly.

It's pretty inconvenient sometimes when Angel is able to pick up my thoughts. She practically glued herself to Gazzy, and twenty minutes later, everyone was already settling down for the night in our tent. Angel was (at least pretending to be) asleep next to her brother, looking deceptively sweet and innocent. Iggy, a famously restless sleeper, was in a corner by himself.

Fang, Nudge, and I were together, tucked like the others under a treated netting that was supposed to ward off malaria-bearing mosquitoes.

"Don't think about what Angel said," Fang whispered next to my ear. "You have to remember—she's still just a little kid."

"A weird little kid," I whispered back. We were holding hands; our feet were entwined.

"Besides," he began. "If she's right...well, I'm glad. It *has* to be me first. Not you."

"Fang, *don't*—"

"Go to sleep," he broke in, then lightened up. "Long

day tomorrow. Starting with your fascinating breakfast." I could barely make out Fang's grin in the darkness—without raptor vision, I wouldn't have been able to see a thing.

"Yeah," I said wearily. A few minutes later, I felt a subtle relaxing of Fang's muscles that meant he'd joined the sleeping flock. I was still wound up, though my body was crying out for sleep. I just kept running over everything in my mind.

Fang—dead. It was unthinkable. A year ago it would have been the worst thing that could happen, and now—it was a thousand times worse. Now I knew what it felt like to hold him, what it felt like to kiss him until we were both breathless. How could I possibly go on without him?

The really, truly horrible thing was, Angel had never been wrong. Never, ever.

12

I WAS STILL AWAKE hours later when a tiny noise made my gaze jump to the nylon wall of the tent. There was a shadow moving there—a person, barely silhouetted against the canvas by the fire. Maybe as close as ten feet away.

I let out a breath of relief. The idea of a mere human lurking around at night seemed like fun 'n' games compared to, say, a hungry lion. I'd not yet been clued in to the wildlife in these parts, and my imagination was fired up. I was definitely not a fan of injury by teeth. Give me a bullet any day.

But then the person stopped and seemed to turn toward our tent. It was a short figure, thick bodied and bulky—pretty much the exact opposite of everyone I'd seen in this country so far. I scanned the silhouette. One of its arms was raised, as if it were holding something, but I couldn't make out the shape of a gun.

Every nerve came to life, and I tensed, ready to give the alarm and wake the flock.

Carefully, I untangled myself from Fang and lifted Nudge's hand so I could slip out. My eyes stayed glued to the silhouette as I made my way to the tent's opening. In one swift motion, I yanked the zipper and burst out.

There was no one there.

After a quick glance around, I jumped and shot out my wings, rising about fifteen feet into the air with a few powerful strokes.

There! Emerging from a ragged stand of trees was that figure again. Raptor vision allowed me to see more detail at night than most people could, but I still couldn't believe what my brain was telling me.

Chu?

He was one of the most evil wack jobs I'd encountered lately. But that was back in Hawaii. He'd been dumping radioactive waste into the ocean. What was he doing *here*?

I landed as silently as possible in a nearby tree. He was speaking in a hushed voice. Must have had a cell phone.

"Yes.... Collecting the new subjects...Approximately fifteen minutes." He disappeared into a small tent with a FIRST AID sign outside. It couldn't have been big enough to hold more than about ten people.

So imagine my surprise when, over the next fifteen

minutes, I saw maybe a couple dozen figures—who appeared to be mostly young-looking refugees from the camp—entering that tent....

And no one came out.

My curiosity got the better of me, so I left the tree and quietly crept behind the tent. No sounds inside. Not even a breath. WTH?

Swiveling my head around to look for more figures, I tiptoed toward the front. Still silence. There was nothing to do but stride right in, striking my best martial-arts pose as I whipped through the tent flap.

It was empty inside.

So...either I was hallucinating or there was a passage to hell underneath this tent. I had to admit I wasn't quite ready to accept either option right now.

Frowning, I returned to our own tent, where I picked my way through a cozy tangle of bird kids. I crawled back in between Fang and Nudge, and took Fang's hand again.

He blinked sleepily, awakening at the slight touch. "Everything okay?"

"Mmm," I grunted. "Go back to sleep."

I couldn't lie to Fang.

13

PICTURE A SHANTYTOWN made of ragged nylon tents, like, for acres. Then picture making a left and finding yourself in front of the big top of the Big Apple Circus. That's what Dr. G-H's crib was like. It was an ornate, beautiful tent, complete with screened windows, a covered porch, and a strip of green carpet leading across the sand to the front entrance.

I glanced at Angel, and she gave me a weak smile. We were both still upset about what had happened yesterday, when I'd lost my cool. That morning Fang had told me not to pursue it, and part of me, I admit, just didn't want to know. I was hoping it would all just go away, so for now, I'd decided to pretend it hadn't happened.

The tent door was pulled aside by a...a guy in a

white uniform who opens the tent door. What a job description.

Inside, netting-covered windows let in light, and electric fans kept the warm air circulating. The floor was covered by Oriental rugs, overlapping so there were no gaps. Our feet sank into soft plush, and I almost sighed.

The doctor came into the "room" from behind a screened-off portion of the space and welcomed us with open arms. "Come, sit," he said, once again looking fashionable and elegant. "You must be hungry. I can't tell you how delighted I am to finally make your acquaintance. I've been following your history avidly."

After glancing around, memorizing exits, I sat down on a leather stool beside a low table. Angel sat across from me, not next to me. I tried (unsuccessfully) not to put too much meaning into that.

"Following our history? Do you know Jeb Batchelder?" I asked.

He looked at me blankly. "Ah, no—no, I can't say I've had the pleasure. Is he a friend of yours?"

"No."

A servant came in with a silver tray piled high with food: pastries, a pitcher of fresh juice, sliced fruit, eggs, *bacon!* I thought of the mush the rest of the flock was eating, not to mention the mush that the entire refugee camp was faced with day after day, and tried (unsuccessfully) to feel guilty. "Please, help yourselves," said Dr. G-H. "You probably require a great many calories, do you not?"

"I know *I* do."

My head swiveled as Dylan came into the room. His dark honey hair was wet, and he looked clean and fresh, which put him two large steps ahead of Angel and me. I almost expected a photographer to leap through the tent flaps, telling Dylan to work it.

"Hello, Max, Angel," Dylan said, sitting on another stool. "Wow, last night seemed like a dream. I couldn't really believe that you existed. And now here you are. And I'm not alone." His face was open and sincere, his expression as clear as his tanned skin. I felt my cheeks flush, no doubt from the first-class cup of joe I'd just gulped.

"Have some strawberries," said the doctor, pushing a silver bowl toward me. He smiled. "There's more where they came from, so don't be shy."

Not really something he needed to worry about, with us. I slathered butter onto a scone, piled orange marmalade on top of that, and took a bite so I wouldn't have to say anything right away. But then I couldn't stand the awkward silence.

"What lab are you from?" I asked Dylan abruptly, with my mouth half full. Miss Manners I am not.

Dylan's perfect brow wrinkled. "Just some lab, up in Canada. I was—I was um, cloned, from another Dylan. Who died in a car wreck or something." He took a bite of pain au chocolat.

I blinked. Most of the clones I'd seen were robotic. Like

44

bad special effects in a movie. Which Dylan most certainly was not. "How old are you?"

"Um, about eight months, I think," he said, looking to Dr. Gunther-Hagen for confirmation. The doctor nodded. "There's been a lot to learn. Like, I suck at flying. I suck at a lot of stuff, actually." He chuckled weakly and looked down at his plate sort of embarrassed-like. I kind of felt sorry for him.

And then felt angry and suspicious. We didn't know him from Adam. This could all be part of an elaborate trap.

This isn't a trap, Max.

I almost dropped my scone as my Voice suddenly spoke up for the first time in ages. Some people have a conscience. I have a Voice. An annoying, buttinsky, intrusive Voice—

Calm down, Max. Relax and enjoy this. This is a special occasion. You see, Dylan is for you. He was designed for you. He's your perfect other half.

14

I INHALED AND ACCIDENTALLY sucked scone crumbs down the wrong way, setting off an apoplectic coughing fit that had the doctor patting my back hard, looking concerned.

Made for me? My perfect other half? Are you freaking insane? my mind screamed, even as my eyes watered and I coughed and coughed, unable to bear the awful tickle at the back of my throat.

"Here, drink this," said Angel, handing me some juice.

"Can you breathe?" the doctor asked. "Do you need the Heimlich maneuver?"

"Heimlich me and die," I managed to choke out, trying to take a sip.

Dylan had frozen, a cluster of red grapes in his hand.

His eyes were wide and watchful, as if he actually gave a crap about what happened to me.

I'd suspected the doctor had an agenda—'cause nothing was ever given to us just because we were swell. Now I knew that it was sitting across from me, looking like the cover of *People* magazine's Sexiest People issue.

"Are you okay?" Dylan asked.

I nodded and took a deep breath. Time to make like a tree and leave. I got ready to stand up.

Max—don't run away. Stick this out. Don't be a coward.

I almost started choking again. Stupid Voice.

"Well, if you're only eight months old," said Angel, "it'll take you a while to learn stuff." She ladled some eggs onto her plate and tucked in. I gave thanks that she was remembering to use utensils.

Again Dylan focused his eyes, the color of the Caribbean, on me. I felt like it was about 110 degrees in there, and took a swig of cold juice. Maybe I had time for another croissant.

"Maybe you could teach me . . . some stuff," said Dylan.

"Max is a good teacher," Angel said with conviction. It made me feel worse about going off on her yesterday. She didn't make up her pronouncements—just reported 'em.

"That's an excellent idea!" said Dr. G-H. "Max would be the perfect person to teach you, Dylan."

"Oh, well. I don't know," I said. "Like what?" *Do not get yourself sucked into this, Max,* I told myself.

"Could I see . . ." Dylan hesitated, then his face hardened

with determination. "Could I see your wings? I've never seen anyone else's."

I thought about saying, *You show me yours and I'll show you mine,* but I'd already seen his. I pushed a couple strawberries into my mouth and stood up. After making sure I had enough space—and I did, which shows you how big the Wonder Tent was—I shook my shoulders a little and unfolded my wings.

Both Dylan and Dr. G-H stared.

"They're beautiful," said Dylan, sounding kind of hoarse. "You really do have them...like me."

I folded my wings and sat down, feeling weird but not knowing why. "Actually, Dyl, *you* have them like *me.* I've had mine for fourteen years. Or so."

A smile played around Dylan's symmetrical features. "Yes. I guess so. Either way, your wings are incredible. They're perfect."

Now I was really uncomfortable, and slathered some butter onto my fourth croissant. Suddenly I just wanted to get out of there, to get back to the others. I'd been sneaking food into my pockets, and my jacket probably weighed several pounds by now. I took one last bite and stood up again.

"Well, this has been fabulous," I said, my mouth full. "But we better get going and perform more humanitarian aid."

"Please, stay," begged Dylan.

"Sorry, no can do," I said briskly.

"Max, we have so much more to talk about," said Dr. Seersucker pleasantly.

"Duty calls," I said. "Ange?"

In a smooth movement, the doctor stepped between me and the tent's entrance. Reaching into his shirt pocket, he whipped out a syringe. "Just a minute, Max. It's not that simple."

15

I SMILED MY EVIL itching-for-a-fight smile, wishing I hadn't stuffed my pockets with bacon. This could get messy.

"Max—wait," Angel said. "He doesn't mean us harm."

"And you know this beca—," I began sarcastically, then realized that she probably did actually know that. Dylan had a familiar alertness, a tensing of muscles that made me wonder if he'd been trained for battle. I guessed I would find out.

"Angel is right," said Dr. G-H quickly. "This is my clumsy way of demonstrating."

"Demonstrating what?" I was barely able to keep a snarl out of my voice. "How to get yourself beat up in one easy step?"

"No," said Dr. G-H. "Demonstrating the wonders of modern science. Watch."

And with that he rolled up one sleeve and swiftly injected *himself* with the hypo. It was something new and different, to watch a scientist experiment on himself. I liked it.

Within moments the doctor gasped, wide-eyed, sucking in breath. He groaned and staggered a bit, holding his throat, then sank down into a chair.

Angel was eating a banana and watching him avidly. I sent her a question: *What's going on?*

She looked at me and shrugged. *No clue.*

I sat down and snagged another cup of coffee and a muffin, since it looked like this might take a while.

For several minutes the doctor hunched over, grimacing. Then he managed to speak in wheezy gasps. "I've injected...a rare strain of virus...that is...going to cause a rather...shocking reaction."

"What you science types do for fun," I said with false cheer. Having grown up in a lab, I associated the words *rare virus* with hazmat suits. I wanted out of there.

He frowned. "Clearly not for fun. But for progress. Sometimes progress is...painful. Now, watch."

Sweat broke out on his brow, and his face turned bright red. And get ready for this most horrific next part, kids: All at once, his skin erupted in grotesque pustules.

I jumped up. "Outta here, dudes!"

"No, wait, Max!" he gasped hoarsely. "The miracle is about to begin."

The only reasons I didn't do an up-and-away were (a) it's hard in a tent, and (b) when I did a double take, I saw that the doc's pustules were already shrinking.

Could I have imagined it? I sat back down shakily.

"To explain it in very basic lay terms," he went on, more quickly now that he wasn't gasping for air, "a number of my organs and systems—including the skin, brain, blood cells, thyroid, the entire immune system—are now working together to analyze the virus, produce the white blood cell and glandular response that will eradicate the virus, and circulate it through my body—almost instantaneously."

"Okay. I can see how that might come in handy," I said, thinking about the sick refugees I'd seen in the camp. "Especially if it puts doctors like you out of business. I don't trust doctors."

The doctor smiled. "You're getting the picture, Max. Because in an apocalypse, there are no doctors. There are no hospitals and certainly no insurance companies. You are on your own. It is you against the forces of nature, which at this point in Earth's history surely see it as in their best interest to eradicate the human race. Do you understand what I mean, Max? Let me give you another example."

He pulled out a meat cleaver.

16

BEFORE I HAD A CHANCE to disappear—fast—Dr. Gunther-Hagen had hacked off the tip of his left pinkie finger.

You heard me right.

Angel screamed. I screamed. The madman screamed too, in pain, then regained his composure.

"Don't worry, children," he grunted. "My biological healing system...is now working together with an advanced stem cell response. I'm able to reposition my severed fingertip"—he moved it back into place and pressed it to his stub, with a pained expression—"or, even more miraculously, were you willing to stay with me for the next several days, you could actually watch a new one grow right back in its place."

"Whoa" was all I could say. Dylan looked unmoved by the whole thing. Guess people sprouting new limbs was common where he came from.

A moment later the doctor held up his left hand and wiggled all five fingers—intact. This guy was seriously starting to worry me, and I began to back slowly toward the door, ready to leap out of the way if he lunged at me with a needle. Or a meat cleaver.

Angel looked excited, and I frowned. Typical yin-yang response from us.

"Okay, I think I get it," I said. "I also get that it all seems a little too good to be true."

"What makes you say that?" the doctor asked, examining his healed finger with satisfaction.

"Well...that must be some pretty super-mega-powerful body chemistry happening there. If it can kill a virus in a single explosion...could it, say, accidentally kill *you*? Or could you accidentally grow an ear instead of a fingertip? How about a claw?"

The doctor waved his hand impatiently. "Of course there are bugs that need to be worked out. Certainly, overactive autoimmune response can be a tricky business, among other challenges. We're working on that, but in the meantime we have the pharmacology to counteract the side effects. My point is that once those bugs are solved, a world of possibilities opens up."

And a world of unpredictable chaos, I thought.

"After the apocalypse, we could all be living like

cavemen again," the doctor said. "We could be hunted by huge mutant carnivores, things we can't even imagine now. We need every weapon, shield, and protection in our arsenal. And here's the important thing, Max. Remember this if you remember nothing else: *We must be our own weapons.*"

His eyes were focused intently on me. I'll just ask now: What is it about my persona that draws every insane, power-hungry nutcase to me like a *magnet?*

"We will have to survive on our own strengths. You can fly. You and the flock have gifts. Dylan here is also gifted, and in some ways different from you. But this kind of healing ability will be the difference between life and death in the near future."

"Wow," I said. Traditionally, I would have come up with something snappy and/or scathing here, but I have to tell you, this guy unnerved me.

Because, in a crazy way, what he was saying made some degree of sense.

"It's . . . really impressive," I said. "But I don't see what it has to do with me, with us."

Dr. G-H straightened. "I asked you here to discuss a possible alliance between us—a partnership, if you will: your flock and my companies, me, and Dylan. With your natural abilities and the powers of science I'm unleashing, we can, in essence, ensure the survival of humankind."

"We would be allies?" Angel asked.

"No," I told her, giving her a warning look that she ignored. Again, I started to make my way toward the door.

"You six are the most successful recombinant-DNA life-forms ever created," Dr. G-H went on earnestly. "Until now." He motioned proudly to Dylan, who had the decency to look embarrassed. "My companies are producing some of the most cutting-edge, daring science in the world today. Together, we could actually achieve your mission—to save the world."

I stopped in my tracks and turned back to face him. Okay, he had insider info.

"Sorry. Thanks for asking. But the flock works alone." I was acutely aware of Dylan's steady gaze, his tightly coiled tension as he watched the doctor. "Thanks for the great breakfast," I added. "I'm really impressed with your science and all. But I don't think we're the right partners for you."

That was probably the most diplomatic, least obnoxious reply I'd ever given anyone in my whole life.

"This isn't good-bye, Max." The doctor's voice followed me as I exited the tent. "And that isn't your final answer."

17

DID I EVER TELL you how much I hate needles? Bad childhood memories. It's a lab-escapee thing. The meat cleaver was a mere annoyance in comparison.

My mind was still reeling as I slogged through the sand back to our camp. I kept a death grip on Angel's hand as she trotted beside me to keep up. The African sun beat down on us, and for the first time, the heat felt crushing to me.

I really wanted to help the CSM and the refugees here, but my Mother Teresa aspirations were crumbling fast. This place was suddenly way too dangerous for us. Angel's dire prediction, what the Voice had said about Dylan, Chu and the disappearing refugees in the middle of the night, and now Dr. Hans's obsessive fondness for wielding knives and needles full of pathogens had all combined to turn this trip into a nightmare.

We had to get out of there and far away from Dr. Cleaver. ASAP.

"What did you think about Dylan?" Angel asked.

"Poor sap," I said briefly, and tried not to think about him too much in case she was in mind-reading mode.

"Don't you think we should stay and help him?"

"Help him do what?"

"Help him learn," she said. "He's brand-new. He doesn't have anyone else. I don't think he can learn what he needs to know from Dr. Hans. At least we all have each other." She smiled up at me somewhat tentatively.

Stopping, I looked into her blue eyes. "Do we, Angel?" I asked softly, as her smile faltered. "Do we all have each other? Have each other's backs?"

She didn't say anything, and then we were in sight of our tent. Gazzy called over to us. I strode forward and motioned everyone inside. In the heat of the day, it was stifling, but I would make this fast.

"Okay," I said. "First, here." I handed out squashed bacon, muffins, fruit, everything I'd been able to stuff into the cargo pockets of my pants and my jacket. In retrospect, the handful of scrambled eggs had not been a good idea, but still, my poor hungry flock fell on everything like hygiene-challenged hyenas. Gazzy actually moaned as he downed a piece of bacon in two bites.

"Listen up," I said urgently. "It's time to round up your

gear. I'm gonna check in with Patrick, and then we're getting the flock out of here." Ha-ha. "If we head north-northeast, we'll hit Italy. From Italy to Ireland. Ireland to New York. Sound good?"

They all looked at me.

"I'll explain on the road, but we have to get out of here, fast." I even looked over my shoulder, as if Dr. Hacker-Hagen was about to pop through our tent flap.

"Aren't we supposed to stay and help?" Nudge asked, brushing off crumbs.

"We've helped. We've posed for pictures," I said, shoving my stuff into my backpack. "Us staying a bit longer won't do that much more."

"Are we going on another CSM mission?" Nudge asked.

"Nah. At least not for a while," I said. "We're headed someplace new and different—"

Fang looked at me and smiled. It was time to spill our little secret.

"Home."

BOOK TWO

HOME IS WHERE THE HEART BREAKS

18

LESS THAN A WEEK LATER, Iggy was working his magic in the kitchen, with real groceries that we'd bought from a real grocery store. He came out, a chef's hat on his head, big oven mitts on his hands. "Come sit down," he ordered. "Dinner's ready."

Gazzy raced to the table. "Lasagna! Excellent!"

I stood at an open window, looking out over the blood-red canyon, turned to flame by a glorious sunset. We were home. Colorado, that is, where we had lived, post–dog-crate but pre-world-saving-mission. We had a new house there, near where we had lived before. The CSM had built it as a big thank-you for our help in Antarctica and Hawaii.

I had missed these mountains, these gorges. Jeb had brought·us here, about five years ago, after he'd kidnapped us to protect us from the mad scientists at the School. Now I was hoping Dr. Gunther-Hagen never found us here. That would have been a little *too* familiar.

A small black head nudged my leg, and I looked down to see Total smiling up at me. I dropped down to my knees and hugged the furry, Scottie-like body close. "You had a good visit with my mom?"

"Super," he said. Yes, Total can talk—another advantage to being genetically engineered, if you're a dog. "I helped out in her office. And Akila loved it."

My mom is a veterinarian, when she's not trying to solve global problems through the CSM. And Akila is Total's...girlfriend. She's a (non-English-speaking) malamute that we met on our first mission. They're a match made in a carnival sideshow, but they seem happy. "Yeah? What'd you do?"

Total puffed himself up. "Counseled patients," he said importantly. "It helps that I speak their language."

"I bet. Let's go—before Gazzy eats that whole lasagna. I'm starving." Total's small black nose twitched, and we both trotted to the kitchen, where yummy smells wafted toward us.

Fang sat down next to me at the table and quietly linked his ankle around mine. Total hopped up onto a chair between Fang and Nudge.

I dug in to the lasagna, which smelled like heaven, if heaven were hot and cheesy and layered with noodles and red sauce. And maybe it is.

I looked around at my family, the six of us, Total, and now Akila, all sharing a meal together. We were here, far from everyone else. Far from anyone who could hurt Fang. Far from Dylan and Dr. Gummy-Häagen-Dazs. I felt almost like weeping with joy.

I knew it wouldn't last. It never does.

19

THE NIGHT WIND CAME in my open window. I lay in my bed, staring at the ceiling. Somehow, being back in this just-like-the-old-days setting was giving me nasty flashbacks.

I thought about how Jeb had taught us everything he'd known and then suddenly disappeared. We'd been sure he was dead. After a couple years living on our own, the first nightmare in recent history: Erasers—a human-wolf hybrid—had come. They'd attacked us, destroyed our house, and kidnapped Angel. Now that we were back in Colorado, a sense of unease rattled me. I felt as if someone were watching me. Someone with a night telescope?

I shook my head. *Must tamp down the paranoia.*

As if on cue, I heard a sound from outside. Like a slight

scratching. In seconds, I had rolled out of bed, crouched by the window, and quickly peered over the sill.

Nothing. The sky was clear. No one was scaling the wall; no one was rappelling down from the roof.

But there was that sound again. It was closer. My breathing sped up, and my hands curled automatically into fists. Then I saw the doorknob of my room turn very, very slowly. Crap!

My muscles coiled, tightened. . . . A hand crept around the edge of the door, easing it open. I almost gasped. It was an Eraser's paw. I was sure of it. Huge, hairy, tipped with long ragged claws. I still had scars on one of my legs from claws like that. I slithered toward the door, kneeling behind my desk.

A dark shaggy head poked around the edge of the door. I leaped up—then froze.

"Fang?" I whispered.

My eyes whipped down to his hand on the door. It was just a hand. No claws. I blinked several times.

"Sorry," Fang whispered. "Didn't mean to startle you. Trying to be quiet."

I sat down abruptly on my bed, my heart pounding.

"You okay?" Fang soundlessly shut the door and came to sit next to me. "You look like you saw a ghost."

I shook my head, speechless for a second.

"How come you're awake?" Fang whispered, taking my hand in his own non-paw.

I shrugged. "Couldn't sleep. I feel like something's sneaking up on us. Watching us."

"You think Dr. G-H knows where we are?"

"I don't know," I said. "He warned me—he said *no* wasn't my final answer. I keep feeling like he's coming after us, that he'll keep asking me to join forces with him until he forces me to say yes."

"Over my dead body," Fang said, and I flinched.

"Not funny to use that phrase anymore, Fang," I warned him, then continued. "I can't stop thinking about Jeanne too. He's clearly been experimenting on her. Which means he's probably experimenting on everyone at that camp. And Chu is involved. I saw him gathering subjects in that first aid tent. It's so totally Nazi-scary. For one thing, can you imagine an accidental outbreak of one of his 'rare viruses'?"

"He could definitely do some damage," Fang agreed.

"And that's just for starters. People there are desperate, Fang—they'd agree to anything as long as there was a decent meal at the end of it. Lots of those kids are orphans. Who would miss them if something went wrong?"

"You think we should go back?" Fang asked.

"No!" I answered, a little too quickly. "I know; it's pathetic. One day I'm Mother Teresa, and the next I'm all about *me-me-me* again. Us, I mean." Fang nodded. "The problem is, I don't have the slightest idea how to help those people." I sighed. "This guy is an evil genius. Most of the people we've dealt with are evil *non*-geniuses. I'm not sure how to handle him. He's the kind of person who's so brilliant, he probably *could* destroy the entire world."

"So do we tell the CSM? The president? The *New York Times*?"

"I don't know," I said slowly. "I've been going back and forth on that all week. I can't think about it anymore right now," I said, suddenly feeling tired. "Hey, why'd you come in here, anyway?"

Fang's too-long black hair fell over one eye. "Just checking on you. You've been getting wound tighter every day."

"I guess I have. I just...don't know what to do, and I feel like I don't know enough about anything to figure *out* what to do."

"It'll come to you," Fang said confidently. "For now, why don't you try to get some sleep? I'll stay till you're out, if that'll help."

"That would help a lot," I admitted.

I collapsed sideways on my bed and pulled the blanket over me. Fang sat at my side, holding my hand and rubbing my back between my wings.

20

FANG WAS RIGHT. It came to me. The next day I presented my plan to the flock.

"You want us to *what?*" Gazzy stared at me with horror.

"I want us to learn more," I said. Plus, I needed a big project to focus on. "I've been thinking about this since Africa. We know some stuff—how to hack computers, break locks, et cetera. But I've realized there's a lot we don't know. And here we are, living peacefully in our new house, tons of time to spare, hours to fill up—so we should be putting that time to good use!"

"What do we need to learn?" asked Iggy.

"Oh, I don't know.... Like, why was Chad in such a mess? Why were the locals suspicious of Americans?" I paced up and down our living room. "And where did the Romans go, and how did they get replaced by Italians? I mean, the *Greeks* are still around!" I went on enthusiastically. "There's so much to learn. It's never bothered me till now—we always knew enough to get along. But now I'm thinking, How can we fight evil scientists without understanding science? How can we save the world if we hardly know anything about it?"

"We don't have to know about something to save it," Iggy argued. He had one foot on a window ledge, ready to jump out. "I mean, we *know* evil scientists really well, but we don't want to *save* them."

"Okay, that example doesn't even make sense," I said. "But, like, these CSM missions we've been on—we've relied on other people to tell us what we need to know. Mostly, we've been able to trust them. But what if they weren't trustworthy? What if we knew enough to judge for ourselves? We could stay totally independent!"

Fang stroked his chin the way he did when he was thinking. Nudge was staring at me, and now she threw a couch pillow at my head. Only my lightning reflexes kept me from getting a face full of corduroy-covered foam.

"We've had so many chances to go to school!" she wailed. "But *noooooo!* You always *hated* school! You didn't *want* us to learn stupid boring school stuff!"

"I still don't like *school*," I said. "But we can learn by ourselves. We can do field trips. Experiments. There are online courses. We have the computer." I pointed to our super-duper contraband computer, lifted from the government some while back.

"I say no." Iggy folded his arms and looked defiantly at a spot by my left ear.

"I say no too." Gazzy folded his arms, imitating Iggy.

Angel looked thoughtful but didn't say anything.

"We need to do this, guys," I said. "We'll get bored if we just sit around all the time."

"I'm happy to sit around all the time," said Gazzy. "I don't mind being bored."

"Anyone who does not feel the need to deepen his or her font of knowledge is welcome to be on bathroom and kitchen duty for a month," I said. "Are there any questions?" Eyes met mine with various expressions of anger, resentment, uncertainty, yada yada yada.

There were no questions.

21

DYLAN WAS STARING into my eyes. Hard. He was leaning toward me.

"Dylan, no—stop."

His hands were on my shoulders, pulling me closer. "Max, stay," he said. "I know it's hard for you to understand. Or accept. But we were made to be together. You need me."

I edged away but couldn't disconnect from his eyes. "I already have everything—and everyone—I need," I told him. I tried to sound sure of myself. It was clear that Dylan wasn't fooled by anything.

"No," Dylan murmured, almost sadly, as if he wanted to break the news to me gently. "You do need me, Max. I can help you more than anyone."

"Yeah?" I asked, my voice a squeak. It felt impossible

not to drown in the deep blue of his eyes. His strong hands slipped from my shoulders and curled around my back. I'd never felt anyone close to me like this except Fang. It was uncomfortable—but there were also shivers going down my spine.

"You need me because I . . . I can see things no one else can," he confessed. *"I can see people from across the world, across an ocean. I can see what's going to happen. I can protect you."*

"You don't know me, Dylan," I said, steeling my voice but still totally under the control of his gaze. "I've never needed to be protected."

It was as though he didn't even hear me. He stroked his hands along the tops of my wings, smoothing the feathers softly. "I can see that you and I will be together," he said, no hint of a smile on his unearthly good-looking face. "Forever."

22

"NO," I SAID, APPALLED. "No—that can't be true. I'm not ready!"

"I don't care if you're ready or not." Gazzy's voice, irritated, crept into my consciousness. "Don't forget this was your idea."

My eyes blinked open fast, and I almost leaped into a sitting position. I stared at Gazzy, confused, afraid to look around and see Dylan lounging somewhere, a knowing smile on his face.

Oh, jeez. I'd fallen asleep on the couch. Good lord, my subconscious was doing another number on me. I frowned. At least I hoped it was my subconscious.

"Coming," I groaned, getting up off the couch. We were on day three of our homeschooling program, and so far it felt like I was stuck in the La Brea Tar Pits of higher education. So today we were going to try to get out and "spread our wings," so to speak. On a field trip.

Forty-five minutes later we were reducing altitude, getting ready to land in a park in the closest big city to our house. (I can't reveal more about the locale for privacy reasons, you understand.)

"Why can't we go to the NASCAR track?" Gazzy whined. "I think there's a lot more that we could learn there."

Fang nodded. "Gotta agree with Gazzy on that one. Physics. Geometry. Marketing, Advertising. Sociology."

"You're just lucky I'm not sending you guys to the zoo. You'll take the art museum and love it."

"I just don't get what bird kids need to know about art," Iggy said grumpily. Okay, so Iggy had a good reason to be complaining, what with not being able to see art and all.

"Well, I don't either, to tell you the truth. That's the whole point. There's a reason that people flock to look at a bunch of useless things sitting in a building. We're going to find out what it is."

We landed in a grassy clearing away from the walking paths, then sauntered over to the nearby art institute. "Aren't you afraid someone might find us here?" Nudge asked, looking warily at the school buses pulling up to the parking lot.

"I think an art museum is the last place in the world you'd look to find a bird kid."

The reason? We'd never been to one. Didn't seem like

the place to head for survival. Now that I was actually in one, I saw that I'd been way off base.

Clean bathrooms. Cafeteria. Dozens of deserted corners, galleries, hallways, and back stairs where you could hide for hours, maybe even days. Outdoor courtyards for flying exercise. Huge mega-galleries with two-story-high ceilings that would be great for indoor flying. In an emergency, weapons would be available in the hall of medieval armor. The educational center had computers and books, and the gift shop had cool stuff for the younger kids—puzzles, games, arts and crafts...

Fang interrupted my reverie. "So what's the plan?"

"Stay in pairs," I directed. "Nudge and Angel, Gazzy and Iggy—"

"And Fang and Max," Iggy finished in a mocking sing-songy voice.

I ignored him. "Meet back here at the ticket desk in an hour and a half. And come with answers to these questions." I pulled out a piece of paper I'd jotted notes on earlier in the day. "Okay. Each of you should tell us something you learned about history, about yourself, and about one or more of us."

The flock looked at me blankly.

"We only have an hour and a half to practically discover, like, the meaning of life?" Fang asked.

"Why not? We've had to do harder stuff to survive," I pointed out. "And besides—you never know. Someday we might have only a few seconds to figure out the meaning of life."

23

FOR SOMEONE WHO WAS way more interested in NASCAR less than an hour ago, Fang sure seemed to be getting into the art museum. I mean *way* into.

"Were you, like, Indiana Jones or something in a former life?" I quipped as Fang dragged me through the fifth or sixth hall of ancient artifacts.

"Maybe," Fang said in a faraway voice as he gazed at a birdlike ritual mask made by the—I squinted at the placard—Senufo tribe. We'd been through the Egyptian, Greek/Etruscan, Roman, pre-Columbian, and Native American collections, and now we were into African art.

"Aren't you sick of broken pots and hatchets yet?" I asked him.

"What's your hurry?" Fang turned and looked me in the eye. "Or d'you think that if you can't save the world with it, it's not worth your time?"

"Look, I have to find answers to my own questions or I lose leader credibility. And I haven't found them here. I'm thinking maybe a da Vinci would be useful. He was pretty smart, from what I've heard."

"Don't think so much, Max. This is supposed to be about feeling stuff, not finding answers, right?"

Did I hear him correctly? Fang talking about *feeling* stuff?

Maybe there *was* something special about this place.

I knew Nudge and Angel had started off in the historic-garments gallery, and I figured they'd never leave a room full of eighteenth-century court dresses and Victorian ball gowns. So I was kind of surprised when we crossed paths near the Impressionist room.

"Predictable," Fang whispered. "Pretty pastel-colored paintings of landscapes, flowers, and ballerinas."

Those two were so completely zoned into the pictures that we tiptoed right by them. They didn't even notice. What was it that Angel was so hypnotized by? I casually glanced at the placard to get the artist's name. Mary Cassatt. I saw picture after picture by this painter of beautiful mothers with beautiful children. All soft, warm, comforting.

And I saw a tiny, tiny tear roll down Angel's cheek.

*   *   *

Of all places to run into Gazzy and Iggy: the gallery where the canvases were big and the colors were wild, angry, free, and — well, *explosive*. The security person informed me it was called the "abstract expressionism" space.

"What are you guys doing here?" I asked. "Thought you'd be in the armory."

"Well, it's the easiest place for me to describe what I'm seeing to Iggy," Gazzy explained.

"You've gotta be kidding," Fang said, pointing to a painting made up of random splatters and lines. "Seems like the *hardest* place to be describing stuff. 'Cause there are no...actual...pictures here."

"I can detect color fields, remember?" Iggy reminded us. "And then Gazzy just makes up the rest. What he thinks the picture represents."

"Yeah, like that one over there?" The Gasman gestured to a composition that looped and splashed around two yellow circles. "It says *Untitled #5,* but I call it *Happy Breakfast:* Take two gigundous sunny-side up eggs, stomp on the yolks, then dance around a little bit with an open bottle of ketchup in one hand and a can of motor oil in the other." Iggy nodded like it made complete sense.

It was sweet of Gazzy to interpret, but God, did I wish Iggy could see with his own two eyes.

"Okay, everyone, time to report," I announced.

I still didn't have answers to my own questions, but one

of the good things about being the leader is you can some-times get away with not doing your own assignments. "Who wants to go first?"

Nudge, the eternal good sport, volunteered. "In the garment gallery we learned about corsets. Ugh! Max, did you know that they could *squeeze* people to death?" Hmm, I should've restricted undergarments from the assign-ment. "I also learned that Angel can't stand to look at any pictures with bad stuff in them, like devils or people or animals getting killed. Including dragons," she went on. "And, um, about myself, I learned I like the photography the best. Imagination is great and all, but I like real people more."

"A-plus, Nudge. Extra credit for that surprising insight on Angel." Angel gave me a look like I was being mean. She was probably right. "Gazzy?"

"In the armory I learned the earliest gunpowder formula—coal, salt, pepper, and sulfur—and it was first written down in the year 1044." I was pretty sure Gazzy already knew every formula for every explosive in history, but oh well. "And I decided that Iggy sees a lot less than he lets on. Also, I learned that I have a good imagination."

"Sure you do, Gazzy, but didn't we all know that?" I pointed out.

"If you did, you never told me," he said poutily. *Note to self:* Must do better at encouraging flock.

"Fang? What say you, wise man?"

"Well, did you guys know the Rosetta Stone is, like,

way more than a computer program? It's actually this kind of awesome hieroglyphics-decoder-type rock. And about the flock, I discovered that in some parts of the world, if us bird kids had appeared hundreds of years ago, they literally would have thought we were gods. That's pretty cool. And about me? I realized...I'd really like to travel the world. See different cultures, live in a tribe. I'm thinking Papua New Guinea or somewhere."

"Yeah?" I raised an eyebrow. "Well, have fun with that. I think the flock's seen enough of the globe lately."

Fang flashed me a look of irritation. "Didn't think I was getting graded, Max. Remind me to keep my mouth shut next time. I'll risk the F."

Okay, that was pretty much three strikes in a row for me. "I'm sorry, guys—I guess I'm just jealous that you all discovered this great stuff and I...didn't."

"Whatever, Teach," Iggy said, a little disgusted. "In case you're even remotely interested in hearing what I have to say, I learned something about myself."

"Of course I want to know, Iggy," I said hastily. "What is it?"

"I learned I want to see."

We were all quiet.

Iggy had never said that. We totally took for granted that his superior extrasensory skills seemed to give him pretty much the same abilities and quality of life the rest of us had—if not better.

"I'm sorry, Iggy" was my best response. "I wish I could help you."

"Max? You didn't ask me," Angel spoke up. Another wounded flock member.

"I was just getting to you, Ange. Did you discover anything?"

"Yeah. I found out that the African art collection here is on loan from the H. Gunther-Hagen Foundation. I didn't know the doctor liked art, did you?"

My day was now officially ruined.

24

AFTER OUR ART INSTITUTE DIVERSION, I decided
to go back to normal lesson plans to avoid the element of
surprise—i.e., not knowing answers to my own questions.
Control and I, after all, were *likethis*.

But even normal lessons turned out to be a problem.
Case in point: everything mathlike besides plain math
(+, −, ×, %) was a huge recipe for trouble. Nudge was
reduced to tears by the natural–unnatural number conun-
drum, and tensions were high again.

"Look, I know this has been really hard," I said, "but
we don't just quit because something is hard."

Nudge frowned. "Yes, we do. We do all the time!"

Fang brushed his hand across his mouth and looked
down at the table, obviously trying to hide a smile.

"Well, okay, maybe sometimes we do," I admitted. "But I'm not backing down from this. We're going to be educated if it kills us!" I looked at them seriously. "Because if we're not educated, I'm *dang* sure *that* will kill us."

"Max?" Angel turned her innocent blue eyes on me. "Here's something to learn, but it's funner to read." She pulled out a book and handed it to me. Alarms went off in my head when I saw the cover: *The Way to Survive,* by Dr. Hans Gunther-Hagen.

"Where'd you get this?" I took the book from her and started flipping through it.

"Dr. Hans gave it to me in Africa. It's really interesting," said Angel.

"Okay," I said, narrowing my eyes at her. When was she hanging out with Dr. G-H in Africa? "Class dismissed."

For the rest of the afternoon, I curled up in our deck hammock and blocked out the sound of the TV coming from inside while I read Dr. Scary's book.

Fang came and sat in the other end of the hammock, so our feet were touching. I thought about the last time we'd managed to really be alone—not counting the night I'd thought he was an Eraser, 'cause that had sucked—and my cheeks flushed. I wished we were twenty years old. I wished we were safe and didn't ever have to worry about people like Dr. G. I wished we could do whatever we wanted.

"Whatcha doing?"

"This is what Angel is reading. I'm wondering if the not-so-good doctor got to her in Africa."

"Compelling read?"

"Just kind of horrible," I said quietly. "At first it seems like he's talking about how to save the earth, and how mankind has messed everything up, and how we should fix it. But if you keep going, he says that the only way for humankind to survive is if it radically changes—becomes more than human. He calls it skipping an evolutionary grade. Basically he wants everyone to 'evolve,' and he's trying to come up with the technology to jump-start it. If he had his way, no one would be one hundred percent human anymore. Everyone would be hybrids, or have their genes tinkered with, to make them superhuman."

"We like being more than human," Fang pointed out.

"But we're only more than human because we're rare," I said. "What are we if everyone is like us, or evolved in different ways? What if we become the ones who aren't special enough?"

"Hm," Fang murmured. "So where does the doctor go with his plan?"

I frowned. "He asks for help. From scientists, from volunteers. From people who want to be on the cutting edge of a new world. But meanwhile he's out there injecting people with God knows what—or maybe worse. And not every one of his experiments can be a success. Some of them have to be mistakes. Failures. What happens to those people?"

"He's not going to want anyone to see his failures," Fang

said. "In fact, he's going to make sure no one does. He'll have to get rid of them."

I nodded, feeling sick inside.

"Are you thinking we need to stop him?" Fang asked.

"I'm thinking we need to start with some research."

25

DR. SCARY HAD about 300,000 Google hits. We started wading. The high point was stumbling on a photo of him from grad school, which actually made me laugh out loud. Back in the old days, the doc had a lot of hair. And it was perfectly feathered. Wow. You think you know someone...

But it all went downhill from there.

On around page thirty of our search results, we clicked on a link that looked like gobbledygook—but when the screen cleared and refreshed, it almost made my heart stop. At the top of the page appeared the logotype for the Institute of Higher Living. The rest of the screen was blank except for three boxes for a user name and two passwords.

I hadn't heard anything about the Institute in a long time. We'd busted into one of their facilities and released some mutants once. That's where we picked up Total.

Fang and I exchanged glances. We knew we had to find a way to break in.

"Nudge?" I called, and she came over. Nudge had a preternatural gift for computer hacking and was the only one of us who truly knew her way around this high-octane government computer we'd nabbed a while back.

I couldn't even process the flurry of mouse clicks, screen flashes, dialog boxes going open and shut, and letter-number series that Nudge keyed in to the machine as she tried to hack in. It took her about ten minutes to get access—a long time by her measure—and it took Fang and me twenty more minutes of exploring to find a list of lab reports that sounded like maybe, just maybe, they had the fingerprints of Dr. Hackjob-Wackjob:

Morbid Effects of Autoantibodies on Rodents

Autoimmune Toxicity in Systemic Viral Experimentation on Chimpanzees

Abnormal Cell Differentiation from Induced Pluripotent Stem Cell Experimentation

Cancerous Effects of Viral Reprogramming of iPSCs in Human Adults

Defective Apoptotic Processes and Cell Proliferation in iPSC Experimentation on Human Children

Most of those words I didn't know, aside from the red flags of *cancerous* and *abnormal*—but *human children* was all I needed to feel like throwing up. I almost didn't want to go further. But I drew a breath and forced myself to start reading the first document.

Fang and I stared at the screen.

"Is it just me or does this feel like it's written in Latin?" Fang said five minutes later. We were both so freaked by the scientific mumbo jumbo that we hadn't even clicked to the next page view.

"Latin would be easier to understand than this," I grumbled. "But hold on—see those references in parentheses to 'figure one' and 'figure two' and 'figure three'? It means there are pictures somewhere associated with this paper."

"Well, you know what they say...," Fang began.

"A picture is worth a thousand words," I finished. "Let me just skim through the rest of this stuff real quick and see if anything catches my eye."

I have to give myself credit for that one. Most grown-ups wouldn't have even bothered to try to wade through that crap, but I managed to pick up on two key points.

First: Autoantibodies set your immune system against you and attack the body's own organs like they're the bad guys. Second: Abnormal cell growth, too much cell growth, badly "programmed" cell growth = party invitation to cancer. Great.

I started clicking through the pages of the PDF faster

now, to get to the pictures. And then, when I did, I wondered why I'd been so eager to see them.

Our grisly tour of Dr. Hans Gunther-Hagen's Gallery of Mistakes took at least two hours.

We saw people with purple eyelids and grotesquely bulging eyes the size of baseballs, people with glands in their necks so swollen it looked as if there were an alien creature growing inside them. Others had muscles so inflamed their bodies ballooned and twisted into shapes I didn't think possible. The skin disorders were maybe the worst for me to look at. Rashing and cracking and bleeding and virtual disintegration so wildly extreme that I had to stand up and walk away from the computer at one point.

This was only what was happening on the surface of these victims. I'd read enough to understand the bottom line: toxic disaster. Chronic pain, even agony, not to mention the psychological effects of dealing with it.

"There's more. The regeneration stuff," Fang said, and I nodded. It was a horror show, but I had to go deeper, and deeper still. Page after page, image after image, document after document.

I can't even write down the details of what I saw on the screen that day. It would bring back too many nightmarish visions of festering wounds, partial and deformed limbs, and horrific tumors of all shapes and sizes.

"I just knew it," I said in a low voice. "I knew he would stop at nothing to accelerate his research on humans."

What we would call mistakes, Dr. G called progress.

26

IT WAS HOURS later when Iggy jolted us out of Dr. Hans's Fun House.

"What've you guys been doing all this time? Online poker? You sure are . . . *into* it."

"Playing a video game," Fang answered, hiding the document on the computer desktop. Even though the other kids had seen a lot of freaky stuff in their lives, it was still our instinct to protect them from anything that might overload their quota of nightmares.

"You're lying through your fangs," Iggy accused.

Fang tried to play innocent—but "innocent Fang" is an oxymoron, so it didn't work.

"That reminds me," Angel called over to us from the couch. "I have a video for you, Max!"

She skipped to her bedroom and brought out a backpack that she turned upside down. Out dropped a clogged travel-size hairbrush, an iPod Shuffle, and a CD in a linty transparent sleeve.

"I found it in my bag a few days after we got back from Africa. It has your name on it, but I don't know how it got there—I swear."

I didn't have a good feeling about this, but curiosity got the better of me and I popped the CD into the computer right away. I'd drill Angel later about why she "forgot" to give it to me until now.

When I clicked "play," my not-good feeling got much, much less good.

My favorite finger-chopping foe smiled at me from the screen.

"Hello, Max," Dr. Gunther-Hagen began. I braced myself, as Fang stood behind me with his comforting hands on my shoulders.

You ran out a bit quickly today, and I was so excited to be demonstrating my work that I never had the opportunity to give you some of the more important reasons why I know you would find it very rewarding to work with me.

As I'm certain was apparent from what you saw and learned of my limb-regeneration project, I am the world's leading expert on stem cell research, bar none. Growing an organ in a dish and implanting it is rather an elementary process for me and my team compared to limb regeneration. In fact, I've been successfully implanting organs grown from subjects' own tissue for a number of years. Were you to join forces with me, doors would open up for you and your flock.

He paused dramatically.

"For example, wouldn't one of your boys love" — he reached to his side and slid a cloudy jar into view of the camera — "a brand-new pair of these?"

He picked up the container so the camera could focus on it.

Floating inside was a human eyeball.

27

THE NEXT MORNING I SET the kids to working on independent studies, and I did more computer research about genetic-recombination theory and stem cell science. I knew they had incredible potential to help humankind. But what became clear to me was that the doctor was experimenting way too fast on humans. All my research had done was upset me.

So now I was emerging from a long shower that was supposed to be therapeutic. I started dragging a comb through my brown hair, getting caught in snarls. Really and truly stuck. I got lost in the ritual of trying to untangle the tangles—contemplating Dr. Hans and Iggy and the possibility of new, healthy eyes for one of the people

I loved most in the world—as the moisture on the mirror slowly began to dissipate.

That's when I spotted an Eraser in the mirror, looking out at me through the fog.

Reactions were faster than thought, and I whirled, one fist raised to strike...an empty wall. A fast look showed that unless the Eraser was paper thin and stuck to my back, there was no one in here but me.

I sat on the edge of the tub, heart pounding.

This had happened once before, ages ago. I'd looked in the mirror and seen an Eraser version of Max looking back at me. But Erasers didn't even exist anymore—they'd all been "retired." I peeped up over the edge of the mirror. The steam had cleared, and I saw my human face, my brown eyes.

What was happening to me?

28

SWEARING UNDER MY BREATH, I searched the bathroom, opening cupboards, feeling under the sink. I examined every inch of every wall and ran my fingers around
the window frame. If there was a camera hidden in there,
I didn't find it.

A tap on the door made me jump like a deer.

"Yeah?"

"It's me."

I unlocked the door and let Fang in. Grinning, he
shut the door behind him. Then he saw my face. "What's
wrong?" He glanced around. "You have that ghost look
again."

I let out a breath. "Nothing."

"Then why is a comb stuck in your hair?"

Crap. I slowly pulled it out, trying to get through the worst of the tangles.

From down the hall, I heard raised voices and a crash, and I tensed.

"The kids are taking a little break," Fang said.

"But everything's okay out there?" I tried to sound casual.

He shrugged. "I think they're getting cabin fever." He stepped forward and put his hands around my waist. "But enough about *them*," he said, and his voice sent chills—good ones—down my spine.

I wanted to forget about everything and escape into Fang's kiss. *Don't think, just feel.*

"Where's Max?" I heard Gazzy say out in the hall, and Iggy responded.

"Wherever Fang is, of course." They laughed.

I pulled away from Fang. Even this was being ruined.

"They're okay," said Fang, bending his head again.

A second later I nearly jumped out of my skin, though. "Oh, Fang, you're so haaandsooome," I heard. It sounded like me—standing right next to me.

That was Gazzy, doing one of his absolutely perfect impersonations. He also had a gift for throwing his voice.

"Max! Let me take you away from all this! My darling!" If I hadn't been holding Fang—and also hadn't known that he would never say something that corny—I would have sworn it was him. Cackling laughter.

Fang and I leaned our foreheads against each other.

"Whoa—watch it!" There was a loud crash, and I practically pushed Fang into the wall. Yanking the door open, I strode down the hall.

"What's going on out here?" I demanded, hands on hips.

"Nothing," Gazzy said, smirking. "What's going on *in there?*" He wiggled his eyebrows suggestively, and my face burned. Then I saw it: a pile of broken dishes and leftover food all over the floor.

"Who did this?"

"It was me," Gazzy said in Nudge's voice.

"Hey!" she said. "They were wrestling."

"You're supposed to be *studying*," I snapped.

"Oh, while you get to make kissy-face with Fang in the bathroom?" Iggy sneered. "I don't think so."

I was so mortified I was speechless for a second. Then I stamped my foot and said, "Get back to your books!" Which was, of course, a huge mistake.

29

THEY JUST STARED at me for a moment, then Iggy's face contorted into anger. He yanked off his iPod earphones and threw the whole thing across the room. "I can't take it anymore!"

"Hey!" I said sharply. "Those are expensive!"

"I can't help it!" he shouted. "I've been listening to how the Roman Empire fell, and all I can say is, it didn't fall nearly fast enough!"

"You're, like, totally sucking the fun out of the first kind-of vacation we've had in ages and ages!" Gazzy whined, his arms crossed.

Even Nudge, my peacemaker, chimed in. "I listened to an hour of French history this morning, and I thought my head was going to explode," she said. "It's just, army this, invader that, conquering whatever. We have to learn, and I *love* learning things, but there has to be a better way. *Like at a school!*"

I was shocked—Nudge had always been my most loyal supporter.

Well, I wasn't going to stand for this. I was the flock leader! I was going to restructure our lesson plans, I was going to start issuing demerits or other teachery things, I was going to...

I was going to stop being such a hard nose.

I had an idea, and I like to think it actually came from my own brain and not from the Voice or from Angel. And it's so sad that I even need to clarify that.

"You know," I said slowly, "I'm going to be fifteen tomorrow."

Blank stares. I guess I hadn't made the smoothest segue in the world.

"What?" Iggy asked.

"I'm going to turn fifteen tomorrow," I said, warming to the idea. "It's high time. I can't remember when I turned fourteen. We've got to start writing this stuff down. Anyway, tomorrow I'm going to be fifteen. So we need a party."

"If you get to be fifteen, then I get to be fifteen!" Iggy sounded indignant.

I looked at Fang. "Wanna be fifteen?"

His smile melted me. "Yeah."

"I want to be twelve!" Nudge cried.

"I'm nine! I'm nine!" said Gazzy, jumping up and down.

"I'm already seven, but I didn't have a party," said Angel.

"Then it's decided," I said in my leaderly way. "We're all turning a year older tomorrow, and we're going to have a big party."

My flock cheered and started dancing around the room. I sighed happily.

Sometimes being a good leader is knowing when to . . . back off.

30

"ME AND MY BIG MOUTH," I muttered, looking around my room. "Sure, let's have a party; let's all get a year older! Excellent idea, Max. But what are you gonna do for presents?"

The six of us had never had much, and we'd been on the run, on the road, for so long that we'd been forcibly pared down to having, like, nothing. But I wanted to do this right—'cause what's a birthday party without presents?

I had about twenty hours. I was going to have to improvise. Opening my bedroom window, I climbed onto the sill and looked out over the canyon. I was stopped by a sudden thought.

I knew what I really wanted to get Iggy for his birthday.

And I knew where to get it.

But . . . I just couldn't pay that price. I couldn't.

I leaned forward and let myself drop into the air, enjoying the thrill of free-falling before snapping my wings out and rising.

Let's see the doctor touch the sky!

"Do you think she'd like a bomb of her own?" Gazzy asked Iggy.

Iggy thought. "I kind of don't think so. She usually just relies on us to do all that."

"Well, what can I give her?" Gazzy ran his hand through his hair in frustration. "Bombs are the only thing I know how to make!"

"Well, here's an idea," said Iggy, and leaned over to whisper into Gazzy's ear.

A smile slowly widened on Gazzy's face. He rubbed his hands together. "Brillllliant."

Nudge sang softly to herself as she worked. It had been totally worth it, lugging everything back from Europe and New York. Look at how handy these things were now! Her backpack had been stuffed, and she'd hidden 80 percent of everything she'd bought, sure that Max would make her dump it as being not worth lugging around, a liability in case of a fight, etc., etc., etc. Now it was all paying off.

Two presents down, three to go. She smiled as she reached for the hot-glue gun.

*   *   *

Angel straightened, listening. Overhead she heard the cries of a hawk, and she shaded her eyes to watch it wheel through the sky. She loved flying with hawks. They'd all learned a lot from them. You'd think that flying would be as natural as walking, and it was, in a way, but it was also a skill that could be improved.

Other than the hawks, she was alone in the canyon. She had most of what she needed, but a couple more things would be perfect. Her sharp eyes darted here and there, searching in the shadows, checking out every shape, every outline.

Oh, there! Perfect! It was amazing that vultures hadn't picked the bones clean.

It was just what she needed for the presents she was making.

Fang saw the shine of familiar brown hair way down the street and stepped back quickly into the shadow of a storefront. What was she doing here, more than a hundred miles from home? He smiled: no doubt the same thing he was doing.

So far he was in good shape: He'd gotten a really scary thriller novel on CD for Iggy. It was totally inappropriate for kids, and he knew Ig would love it. For Nudge he'd bought a dozen different fashion magazines, all about hair and clothes and makeup. He could already imagine her squealing with joy, then disappearing for several days to curl up somewhere and pore over every page.

For Gazzy? A history of explosives and how they'd been used in warfare for thousands of years. It was like giving candy to a diabetic, but it was perfect.

Angel had been a bit more difficult. Dolls or games or anything for a little kid just seemed too...young. She'd changed so much in the past year. She didn't even sleep with Celeste anymore, the ballerina bear she'd scammed for, so long ago. And yet, she *was* still a little kid.

He'd finally settled on a camera. And he hoped she would use it for good instead of evil. The first time she rigged it up in the boys' bathroom, he'd take a baseball bat to it.

And for Max—Fang smiled even as his heart began to pound a little harder. He hoped she would like what he got her. He hoped she wouldn't say it wasn't practical or whatever. But with Max, you never knew.

It was one of the things he loved best about her.

31

"IG, YOU HAVE outdone yourself," I said, taking another bite of chocolate cake.

Iggy grinned and cut himself a second slice, which meant there was only about half an acre of cake left, slathered with a couple bathtubs' worth of icing.

"You have to get the right proportion of cake to ice cream," Gazzy said. "Each bite needs cake, frosting, and ice cream, all at once. It's the combination that really makes it." He managed to get his carefully loaded spoonful into his mouth before it dropped onto his shirt. Like the last one had.

"And thank you to Fang for getting the ice cream," I said, waving in his direction. "And the balloons!"

Everyone chimed, "Thank you!" while Fang bowed.

My happy, chocolate-smeared bird kids were relaxed, laughing, having the best time we'd had in—ever. It was the perfect way to celebrate our new house, our new lives.

"Is it present time?" Nudge asked, bouncing in her seat. "I can't wait anymore!"

"Yes," I said, and everyone cheered. So let me see: have party, massive amounts of cake and sugar, presents, etc., and I'm super popular. Insist on schooling, homework, education, and everyone hates me. Okay, got it. "Who wants to go first?"

"Me, me!" Angel jumped up and rummaged in a paper grocery bag, pulling out small packages wrapped in the Sunday comics—one for each of us.

I quickly ripped open the paper on mine, and something small fell into my lap. I picked up a necklace strung on a black silk cord.

"It's a good-luck charm," said Angel. "I made it myself. I found all the stuff outside."

My necklace was weird and beautiful, not unlike Angel herself. "Is this a...snake jaw?" I asked. Angel nodded. The small, sharp fangs of a snake's lower jaw spiked delicately among eagle feathers, bits of worn glass, and some ancient aluminum pop-tops from soda cans.

"See?" said Angel. "It's like you: kind of dangerous but really pretty and strong and unusual. See?"

The bits of glass caught the light and glittered like gems. I nodded, really touched. "Thank you," I said, and gave her a big hug, like old times.

Each of us had a similar but unique necklace, and each necklace really reflected who we were. Fang's was all black obsidian, the top half of the snake jaw, and some eagle feathers. She'd really put a lot of thought and work into them.

"Now mine!" said Nudge, pulling out her wrapped gifts.

I'd never had so many presents all at once, and even though I was a big fifteen-year-old now, I couldn't help feeling excited as I ripped off the wrapping paper.

Nudge had hot-glued all sorts of pretty shells and beads around a picture frame. It was gorgeous, too heavy to lug around, and totally not sturdy enough to survive even a light battle.

"Nudge, it's beautiful! I love it!" I told her. She threw her arms around me, and I realized that she had grown several inches without my noticing.

"Oh, my, gosh." Angel's quiet voice got my attention. I looked over to see her holding a small digital camera, her eyes wide.

"Who gave you *that?*" I exclaimed.

Angel's face shone. "Fang. Oh, I love it so much! I've wanted a camera for so long. The first thing I want to do is take a picture of all of us."

"I can put it in my frame," I said, holding it up. Nudge looked pleased.

"Here," said Iggy. "I made fudge for everyone. Didn't have time to wrap it." He held out a large plate covered with neat squares of marbled chocolate–peanut butter fudge. I figured we had about forty minutes before we were all in sugar-induced comas.

"Max!" Gazzy cried. "Way cool!" He held up his certificate for one tattoo at the tattoo parlor a couple towns over. (No, I'm not going to mention which one.)

"I got one too!" Nudge squealed, waving it around. "I'm going to get a unicorn! Or a heart! Or a rainbow!"

"I'm going to get a stick of dynamite on my arm," Gazzy said.

Okay, it wasn't the most imaginative gift, but I'd been pretty sure everyone in the flock would like a tattoo. It looked like I was right.

Fang came and stood next to me. "This is for you."

He held out a small box tied with satin ribbon. My heart started thumping hard, as if I'd been in a fight. With shaking fingers, I pulled off the ribbon and opened the box.

32

I QUIT BREATHING for a moment when I saw what was inside the box. It was a delicate, old-fashioned birthstone ring, with this month's birthstone.

Every other person in the world would have looked at it and thought, *Max would hate this.* It was girly. It was beautiful. It wasn't made of titanium and black leather with spikes on it. But it seemed exactly right, in a weird, heart-fluttery kind of way. And I really loved it.

Quickly I slipped it onto the ring finger of my right hand. It fit like it was made for me. I couldn't stop looking at it.

I realized that Fang was waiting for a reaction. "Thanks," I managed, my voice husky. "It's perfect."

"You're perfect," Fang whispered, leaning close. "As is."

It took several seconds for me to realize I was beaming at him like an idiot. I shook my head, trying to escape the pull of his gaze.

"Okay, now! Everyone up to the roof!" Gazzy said, clapping his hands. "I can't give you your presents inside! Something might catch on fire."

I had a flash of concern that was quickly wiped out as we all flew up to our rooftop. The sun had just set, and there was a lingering pink glow outlining the mountains in the distance.

We sat down in a line on the roof, our legs dangling over the edge. Even in the dim light, I kept turning my hand this way and that, looking at my ring, feeling like I was glowing inside.

Nudge, sitting next to me, gave me another hug. "A tattoo!" she said happily. "They're so in right now! I can't decide."

"You'll find the perfect thing," I told her, happy that she liked my gift.

"Now, everyone, stay sitting down," Gazzy said, fiddling with something in a big cardboard box. Fang moved behind me and gently pulled my shoulders back so I was leaning against his chest. Of course I started practically hyperventilating. After the flock's teasing, I was super self-conscious, but clearly Fang had no intention of pretending that we weren't—*together.*

"Max first," said Gazzy. "Since it was her idea to have a birthday party."

We all cheered as Gazzy flicked his lighter. Something caught fire in the darkness, and after a few seconds of hissing and crackling, went *whoosh* out into the night. Three seconds later it exploded, making a gorgeous blue fireball of sparks, and we all went ooh and ahh. As the sparks fizzled and began to fall, they looked roughly like the letter *M*.

"Oh, my God!" I cheered. "Gazzy, that's beautiful! How did you get it to do that?"

Gazzy smiled modestly. "I can't tell you that. Next, Fang!"

Fang's fireball was a brilliant orange, lighting up the sky.

In fact, it was so bright that it illuminated the old, unused logging road way below us in the gorge. And it showed a black Jeep four-wheeling it up the side of our mountain.

I got to my feet just as Fang's orange letter *F* appeared. "Flock!" I announced. "We have company."

33

WE CROUCHED DOWN, staying in the shadows on the roof. The moon was bright overhead, and our raptor vision easily picked out the dark Jeep as it came toward us.

"Any chance it's lost? On its way somewhere else?" Fang asked softly.

"Yeah," I muttered. "Sure. It's probably the Easter Bunny and Santa Claus, and they're looking for the North Pole." I shook my head, already pumped into battle mode.

It was starting. I could feel something change. I'd been on edge, paranoid for days. There was too much déjà vu: the house, the location...I'd seen an Eraser paw and an Eraser face. Even the black Jeep reminded me of the first time the Erasers attacked our old house. We'd been on the run ever since.

It was almost like the nightmare of the past year was about to start all over again.

"Okay, guys," I said tightly, "let's fan out. Hide high in trees, watch and see what happens. Check the sky for choppers; make sure the Jeep's sunroof doesn't open. When I give the signal, we attack. Aim for the Jeep's windows. Break 'em."

"Right," said Gazzy, his face determined.

Almost silently, we ran hunched over to the other side of the roof, farthest from the road. I couldn't believe this was happening. We'd barely been at the house a week....

I coiled my muscles, just about to jump—but then Angel cocked her head. "Wait—hold on, Max. I think...it's Jeb."

"Jeb?" Nudge said in disbelief.

Angel straightened and nodded her head. "Yeah, it's Jeb. We don't have to attack him, do we?"

I groaned to myself. As much as Jeb now claimed he was trying to help us, help me, I could never trust him again. It was like he woke up and said, "Oh, today's Tuesday, an evil day." Or "Friday again—guess I'll be a white hat." His shifting loyalties made my head spin.

"Is he alone?" I asked.

Angel looked thoughtful for a moment. "No."

"Great." I sighed. "No, I guess we don't have to attack him. But keep an eye on whoever's with him. It's not my mom, is it?" I asked, suddenly hopeful.

Angel shook her head. "Sorry."

The Jeep pulled up at the base of our house's supports, and I jumped down to the ground to meet it. (You could get into our house only by flying or climbing a long ladder that we let down. Or not. That little design feature had been my idea.)

The driver's door opened, and Jeb got out. At one time he'd been my savior, my teacher, my confidant. Now he was mostly just someone to be wary of—and, apparently, my biological father. But his contributing a cell to a test tube didn't make me all misty eyed and eager to forgive. He would never feel like a father to me—not anymore.

"Jeb," I said evenly. "I guess Mom told you where we were, how to find us?" Inexplicably, my mother still trusted Jeb. And I trusted my mom. Which was the only reason Gazzy wasn't under the Jeep right now, rigging a detonator.

"Yes," Jeb said. "She's getting a team together for another CSM mission—I'll have to tell you all about it later."

The other car door opened, and I braced myself. But instead of, say, Mr. Chu, or a killer robot, or a cyborg assassin, it was something worse: Dylan.

My "perfect other half."

34

JUST BETWEEN YOU AND ME and the lamppost, Dylan could easily be *any* girl's perfect other half. If I didn't already *have* a perfect other half, I might have been thrilled with the gift of my very own gorgeous mutant.

The moonlight glinted off Dylan's dark blond hair, which dipped in a wave over one eye. He wasn't wearing a jacket, and I could see the tops of his wings, a warm chocolate brown, darker than mine or Nudge's.

For no reason I could think of, my heart seemed to thud to a halt. Somehow I hadn't expected to see Dylan again, no matter what the Voice said. I'd left him behind in Africa. Now here he was, *at my home*. Looking at me intently.

Almost as if I were prey.

One by one, the rest of the flock fluttered down from the roof to stand with me.

"What are you doing here?" I asked Jeb curtly. "And how did you get hold of *him*? Are you best buds with Dr. Gunta-Hubunka?"

"I wanted to come see you," Jeb said. "Wanted to make sure the house was okay, that you were settling in, that it seemed safe." He beckoned to Dylan to come closer. "Dr. Gunther-Hagen works in the same field of science as I do. We've crossed paths."

I thought about how the good doctor had said he didn't know Jeb. Did anyone ever just tell the truth anymore?

"Hi, Jeb," said Angel. "Hi, Dylan."

Everyone except me said hi. Not warmly or welcomingly—we're too naturally wary for that—but somewhat civilly. Angel actually smiled.

Having Jeb here was bad enough—a violation of our privacy. And he'd had the gall to bring Mutant-Freak 2.0. *Don't be scared of possibilities, Max,* the Voice said now, just to piss me off. *Don't close any . . . escape routes.*

Huh? Escape routes? How could Dylan be an *escape route*?

"Dylan, you remember the flock," Jeb said, pointing at each of us in turn. "Angel, the Gasman, Nudge, Iggy, Fang, and Max."

Dylan nodded. "I'm really glad to see you again," he said, not smiling. "You're the only ones who are . . . like me." His eyes focused on me again. I looked away.

"Maybe we can come in," said Jeb. "Get caught up."

There was no way I was letting them in our house. It wasn't that I automatically assumed Dylan was evil. The jury was still out on that. But I just didn't get the point of his being here.

And he bothered me. He bothered me a lot.

"Sorry, no can do," I said, just as Fang said, "Sure, what the hey. Come on up."

I looked at Fang. His dark eyes questioned me.

"Yeah, okay, whatever," I agreed ungraciously. I felt as taut as a bowstring and wondered how soon I could get rid of them both.

"Dylan, you can just fly up, like the rest of us," said Fang. "Jeb, we'll put down the ladder for you."

Dylan glanced up at the house's doorway, frowning. Angel and Nudge jumped up and were through the door with a couple of wing strokes. Dylan looked at me again, then at Jeb. "Yeah, okay," he said finally.

He set his jaw, rolled his shoulders a couple times, then gave a jump into the air and tried to flap hard. But he hadn't given himself enough room, and he just thunked back to the earth again, his wings whapping painfully against the ground. Typical newbie.

I heard barely suppressed snickering from Gazzy and Iggy as they flew up onto the porch.

Dylan's chiseled face flushed as he let out a controlled breath and shook his head. "Not as easy as it looks," he said wryly. "I've been trying—"

"Max taught the younger kids to fly," Jeb said. "Max, why don't you take a minute, give Dylan some pointers?"

My jaw all but dropped open. "Oh, he'll get it soon enough," I said, glaring meaningfully at Jeb.

"Yeah, it's okay," said Dylan, acting casual. "It'll just take practice. Max doesn't need to waste her time on this." I wondered if he didn't want a girl teaching him.

Incidentally, other people not wanting me to do something has often been Step One in making sure I do something. Plus, for a minute I actually felt a little sorry for him. It's one thing to be a three-year-old with baby wings and learning how to fly. But this guy was...almost...a *man*. A little pathetic.

"Well, whatever. I can take a minute," I heard myself say.

"Yeah?" Dylan raised an eyebrow and looked at me. He seemed to be trying not to look too eager.

"Yeah, sure, why not?" I said, making a mental note to get a good look at his wings. For all I knew, they were remote-controlled and duct-taped to his back.

"Have at 'im," Fang said easily, and he was on the front porch with an almost silent flutter of his wide deep-black wings. God, Fang's wings were gorgeous. They looked like they belonged on the Angel of Death.

"Good—thanks, Max," said Jeb, climbing the ladder Fang had just lowered, and I indulged in a moment's fantasy about someone slamming the trapdoor on his head.

Then it was just me and Dylan alone out here in the canyon, in the moonlight, and I felt like I was going to jump out of my skin.

"Okay," I said, but my voice came out weird. I gave a little cough. "Let's do this thing."

35

FOR A COUPLE OF SECONDS Dylan and I stood there awkwardly. The night seemed darker and quieter than it had a moment ago. I could smell Dylan's clean scent, like soap and mountain air.

"I thought flying would come naturally to me," he said. He carefully opened his wings and frowned, as if testing their strength.

"Well, it's like walking, or riding a bike," I explained. "It's sort of natural, but you also have to practice."

I remembered Ari, Jeb's son. He'd been a little seven-year-old. Then someone had spliced his DNA with Eraser genes and grafted wings onto him, retrofitting them. The result had been a huge disaster, a Frankenstein.

It looked like they had finally gotten everything right

with Dylan. No one could accuse him of being a Franken-stein. More like Frankenhunk.

I realized what I was thinking and immediately shooed it out of my head. "So, I, uh...," I started babbling. "I guess you flew here...from Africa?" I asked. "Like, in a plane?"

"Yeah. What about you guys?"

"We *flew* flew here. Took about five days. We were pretty whipped afterward. That Atlantic Ocean is a beast."

"That's so amazing." He gazed at me in open admira-tion. "I can't believe how strong you are."

The dream I'd had about Dylan popped into my head in full Technicolor. "Was it hard for you to get used to being big?" I asked, wanting to change the subject. Chitchat is obviously not my best skill. "I mean, I guess you grew pretty quickly."

He shook his head. "I've always been this size. I don't remember anything else. They...made me this way." He hesitated for a moment. "I don't remember being a little kid. I've only been alive for eight months, but it's been long enough to realize that I'm a...freak." He gave a sad little chuckle.

"Well, yeah," I said, not pulling any punches. "So are we. But you've got to remember that *you* didn't make your-self this way. We didn't ask for this to be done to us. Other people did. They knew better, knew they were treating us like lab rats, and they did it anyway. They're the monsters, not us."

"Are you angry about it still?" He looked curious. It was

an odd feeling to have anyone—especially a guy—ask me about my emotions.

"Well, I don't know. Mostly I just suck up what life throws my way, stomp on it, and then keep going. I don't dwell much on what I am or how I got this way. It just is. I just am. I'm Max, and whatever form I take, it's good enough for me."

He smiled. Were those whitening-strip-bright teeth I saw flash between his lips? "It's good enough for me too."

"I didn't ask your opinion on it," I snapped. Ouch. Sometimes I even surprise myself. "Sorry," I muttered.

"Don't be sorry. You're right," Dylan said smoothly. "You didn't ask me. And it doesn't really matter what I think, anyway. I'm definitely a beginner-level freak."

"Well, we've had years—our whole lives—to get used to it and figure things out. You've just been thrown into the middle of it. It's actually kind of amazing that you're not totally freaking out."

You can help each other, Max, said the unwelcome Voice. *You're perfect complements to each other.*

"Shut up!" I hissed under my breath, and Dylan looked startled.

"I didn't say anything."

Gritting my teeth, I nodded. "No, I know. It's just—" I decided to take a risk and stared him down. "I hear voices, okay? If you're gonna be here, get used to it. Or else keep your distance."

If I'd hoped to scare Dylan away from me, he didn't seem disturbed much. "Sure, Max. Whatever."

"Okay, so, flying," I started, taking a deep breath and focusing on the thing I loved most in the world. "Flying is...great. It feels great when you're doing it. It's fun. Pure freedom. There's nothing better."

Dylan smiled, a slow, easy smile that seemed to light up his whole face.

"So the first thing we're going to do," I told him, "is push you off the roof."

36

"HOW DID IT GO?" Jeb asked, when we got inside half an hour later.

"Great!" Dylan reported enthusiastically. "I did it! Max is a great teacher." Before I had time to react, he put his arm around my shoulder and squeezed.

"He's a natural," I said, looking at Jeb and wiggling free of Dylan's arm. "A quick study. Won't need much more help from me." I crossed the room and cut a piece of cake, feeling myself flush.

"The flock has been filling me in," Jeb said. "And I see you all turned a year older today."

"Yep." I took a big bite of cake and perched on the sofa arm to eat it. Clearly Jeb had taken in the remains of the birthday party—the cake, the balloons, the decorations.

Years ago, he'd organized the parties and bought the presents and got the ice cream. Well, he'd given up his right to do that. We didn't need him anymore—not for anything. I hoped it broke his heart. "So, Jeb, why are you *here?*"

"I miss you guys," Jeb lied. I knew him too well. "I wanted to get you caught up on CSM stuff. And I wanted Dylan to see you again, and vice versa. Being with the flock is exactly what Dylan needs. Already, in half an hour, you've taught him more about who he is, what he is, than he's learned in eight months."

"So how did you get a hold of him?" I asked. "I thought he belonged to Dr. Hunca-Munca. You just asked the doc to borrow him for a road trip?"

"I'm standing right here," Dylan said, sounding irritated. "But that's okay. Talk about me like I'm not." He crossed his arms over his chest as Jeb looked at him in surprise.

"That's the tricky part, Jeb," I said snidely. "You guys are always stunned when your little creations, your science projects, turn out to have minds of their own. To want to do stuff for themselves instead of falling into line with whatever you have planned for them." I pointed to Dylan. "He's an actual person. He's *alive.* He's not just a bunch of genes that happen to function! When are you gonna learn? When are you going to quit playing God?"

"I didn't create Dylan!" Jeb protested.

"But you brought him here so our skills could rub off on him, right? What about our skills of *disobedience?*

Independence? Our inability to live in *cages?*" My voice had been rising, and now I realized that everyone else had gone silent. "What if all *that* rubs off on him?"

Jeb rose to his feet. "I got you out of those cages!" he snapped.

"You're also the one who put us in those cages in the first place!" I was fuming. "You always seem to forget that part!"

"And you always forget that I saved your lives!" Jeb yelled. I'd never seen him so angry—none of us had. "Not just once, but over and over! If it weren't for me, you'd be dead by now! If it weren't for me, you wouldn't be alive in the first place!"

The others were staring in shock. Looked like I'd blown our little party to all get-out.

"Which one of us regrets that more, I wonder?" I said, and then I ran to the front door and jumped.

37

I SNAPPED OUT my wings before I hit the ground, and soared up into the rapidly cooling night air. My head was spinning, and it wasn't only because of the four pieces of cake I'd had. Though right now I was regretting them.

I needed answers. I needed someone to say, "This is how it is, without a doubt." Only problem was, who would I trust to tell me that?

You can trust me, Max.

I groaned and rolled my eyes. Perfect. The Voice chiming in now was the perfect thing to push me right over the edge.

Max, if you get pushed over the edge...you'll just fly, right?

I hated it when the Voice said things like that, turned my own words around on me.

Yeah, sure. If one can snarl a thought, and I believe one can, I snarled that one. *But listen, Voice, now that I have your attention—got a question for you: Why is Jeb really here? Why did he bring Dylan?*

The Voice was silent. My mind filled the silence with:

Could Jeb possibly be here to carry out Angel's prediction? To kill Fang?

He'd brought us into this world. I knew he was capable of taking us out of it.

And—had he brought Dylan to replace Fang?

If Dylan was here so Fang could be eliminated, then World War III was about to break out.

I clutched the snake necklace Angel had made for me. Fang wore the matching one around his neck. *He* was my perfect other half.

I know you love Fang, the Voice said now, not answering my questions. *Fang's an amazing guy. But you two have too much history together. Dylan has…potential. Great potential.*

No way! I almost shouted out loud. *I swear I'm gonna kick their butts out of here!*

Jeb has his own reasons for being here, said the Voice. *But I want you to think about Dylan, the possibilities there. He could help you.*

Yeah? Like how? I yelled inside my head.

He has incredible Sight. He doesn't realize it yet. But he can see things happening far away, can see people across oceans—maybe even across time.

I was so shocked I stopped flapping; only the wind yanking my wing muscles up tight made me snap out of it. That was exactly what my dream had been about—Dylan saying that to me.

Max—if you and Fang are together, there's only one flock. But if you and Dylan are together, and Fang is leading a different flock...you're all twice as likely to survive in the event of an apocalypse.

My fevered brain tried to process this. *And who would Fang be with? What other flock? Are there more like Dylan?*

Again the Voice didn't answer me directly. Big surprise. *You and Fang are both too independent. You both tend to solve problems with force, violence. Dylan has different instincts. Which broadens your possibility for survival.*

The Voice was hitting me below the belt, in that it was using reason and patience on me. Totally unfair tactics. I lashed back. *This is too weird and stupid, even for you,* I thought scathingly.

Max—confront your fears, said the Voice. Then it went silent.

38

I WAS STILL about a half mile from home when I smelled smoke. I sped up, and my heart seized as I saw the too-familiar bright flickering of flames coming from inside the house. I swooped inside and skidded to a halt in the foyer.

Our couch was in flames.

Jeb hurried in from the kitchen, Angel right behind him. He had a big mixing bowl of water, and Angel had a juice pitcher. They threw the water onto the couch, where it barely made a dent in the blaze.

"What's going on here?" I shouted as loud as I could to be heard over the din of bird kids yelping at one another. I lunged into the kitchen and grabbed a red cylinder out of the corner. "Any of you ever hear of a *fire extinguisher?*" I screeched as I put out the blaze.

Everyone turned and started yelling at *me,* God only knows why. I covered my ears. "Where's Fang?"

Nudge put her hands on her hips, tears in her eyes. "Isn't he with you?" she asked. "He's always with you."

Just then, to complete my perfect evening, the automatic sprinkler system finally detected the blaze and went off, spraying us all, soaking everything with cold water. I stood there, my hair getting plastered down. The couch sputtered and fizzled and filled the air with the scent of Eau de Wet 'n' Charred Upholstery.

I gave Gazzy my best "You're in so much trouble" glare and went out onto the back deck to look for Fang.

On the deck, I jumped to the railing and balanced there, planning my search pattern. It wasn't long before I could make out Dylan's voice nearby—he was under the house, close to the edge of the cliff.

I jumped over the railing and landed on the ground almost silently. I saw Dylan first, and then, with a flood of relief, Fang. They were standing tensely by a concrete piling. I could tell this wasn't, like, guys' night out.

"This is bigger than you and what you want." Dylan sounded ice cold. It was actually the first time I'd heard his voice like that, and it was unnerving somehow. "I'm telling you, the danger I saw today was real."

Fang's voice was just as cold as Dylan's. "Why should I believe you? We don't know anything about you."

"I get that, Fang. What matters is that *I* know a lot about *her,*" Dylan said. "Probably even more than you do."

Fang's face showed dark fury. I might have witnessed the first bird kid boy fight in history if I hadn't bolted forward, my feet crunching on the gravel. "Fang!"

They swiveled and saw me. Dylan looked taken aback, and Fang's expression was angry and shut.

"The house was on *fire*," I greeted them tersely. "In case you're *interested*."

They both glanced up overhead as if to make sure the house was still standing. Fang sniffed, smelling the smoke, and I saw comprehension cross his face.

"It's out, right?" he said.

I just looked at him.

"Is everyone okay?" Dylan asked stiffly.

"I'm sure you had some super important and *crucial* reason for being out here," I said, my words like icy spikes, "when the living room was going up in *flames* over your *heads*."

"Everything seems under control, Max." Fang shoved his hands into his pockets as he redirected his eyes toward me.

"We were talking about you," Dylan—who hadn't yet learned that honesty isn't *always* the best policy—blurted out.

Fang's gaze sent daggers at him.

I was now ready to crack these two numbskulls' heads together. "Dylan, Flock Rule Number One: The safety of the kids is always most important. Period."

"I understand," Dylan insisted. "But Max, I have to tell you that—"

"And Flock Rule Number Two is, Don't argue with Max or you'll live to regret it." I spun and stomped out to the clearing, turning back for one last jab at Dylan. "And by the way, you clearly *don't* know me better than Fang does. Do you see Fang arguing with me? No, you do not."

Fang rolled his eyes. I jumped up and landed back on the deck.

Advanced life-forms, my sweet patootie. Jerks. Both of them.

39

IT TOOK THE FLOCK about two seconds to correctly read the insane glint of rage in my eye, and they all scuttled out for cleaning supplies while I sloshed around the living room, cataloging damage.

"Max."

I swung my head to see Jeb standing against a wall. Soot was smeared on his face, and his eyes were bloodshot. "Good job taking off like that," Jeb said tersely. "You can't just leave them on their own. And you can't just run away from problems every time you get upset."

"Go jump!" I yelled at him. "How dare you judge me! *You're* the one who left us *all* on our own, when we were much younger than *this!* You *butthead!*"

"Let bygones be bygones, Max. I know we've had our

differences, but we should put them behind us—for the good of the flock." He gestured to the disaster before us. "This clearly isn't working. You need help. I think I should come back and live here. I should take up where I left off."

"Forget it!" I told him in my best voice of authority. "There is no freaking way you will ever live in this house like one of us. I wouldn't trust you if you were the last life raft leaving the *Titanic*!"

"You haven't done much better," Jeb said. "Look at this place! Not to mention how the other kids are feeling so alienated by you and Fang now that you seem to have become your own cozy flock of two."

My face went red. No snappy comeback for that one.

"We never intended for that to happen," Jeb said—like "they" had made a whole flowchart of our lives before we were even born. That was the last straw.

"Guess what? You don't get to *intend* squat to happen in my life, ever again!" I shouted. "You don't get to pick out what freaking *socks* I wear, much less anything else!"

Jeb glared at me. "You're not making good decisions, Max," he said with quiet intensity. "You're being run by your heart, not your head. That isn't how I brought you up."

I thought my chest was going to explode. "You brought me up in a *dog crate*," I said, trying not to shriek. "Those days are over. *Forever*."

40

I HAD NIGHTMARES THAT NIGHT. I dreamed that I slapped Angel, hard, and her head split open—then her face peeled aside to reveal Mr. Chu, my old nemesis. I dreamed that Fang and I were dressed up and walking down an aisle in a church, but when I turned to look at him, he had the head of an Eraser. I dreamed that Ivory boy Dylan had disgusting boils on his face. Eew. I guess my subconscious was trying to make an oh, so subtle point: People aren't always what they seem.

It was late morning when I finally woke, feeling almost as if I'd been drugged. The amount of sun coming in the window told me it was almost lunchtime. I padded down the hall, the smell of smoke and charred couch becoming stronger. When I reached the living room, I stopped in surprise.

It was almost empty. All the ruined furniture was gone. The water had been mopped up. Nudge was on a step stool, spraying the sooty ceiling with cleaner. Without a word, I went into the kitchen for some chow.

Gazzy and Iggy followed me in, carrying dirty dishes and a pile of dirty clothes. Iggy dropped the clothes by the washing machine. When did these guys get so industrious?

"What's all that?" I asked.

"I told them to clean up their pigsty," Angel said. "Gaz, put those dishes in the sink. Iggy, start a load of laundry. Some of your clothes have mold on them."

Was I still having a nightmare? Since when did Angel give orders?

I opened the fridge, but it was empty. I looked around and saw a couple empty cereal boxes, an empty bread wrapper.

"Are we all out of food?" I asked.

"Yeah," said Angel, tapping a piece of paper with a pencil. "I've been making a list. Jeb said he'd stop at a store on the way back from the dump."

"Bless his heart," I said sourly. "But I've always provided the food for this flock. You're all acting like I'm not even here or something." I felt the first prickles of tears starting in the backs of my eyes.

Go figure: I didn't cry when I had my *ribs* broken, but the flock taking care of themselves made me weepy. Angel stared at me.

"Give me the list," I said, trying not to rip it out of her hands. "I'll deal with it. It'll be faster, anyway." Angel pushed the paper over to me. I poured a cup of coffee and sauntered out to the deck.

My chest constricted when I saw Jeb down below. He had a pickup truck with an open-bed trailer hitched to it. Fang was on the trailer, tying down all the ruined, sodden furniture.

Dylan was on the ground, shaking water off books and tossing them into the truck bed. He and Fang were careful not to look at each other.

"Get that lamp, Dylan," Jeb commanded, checking the hitch of the trailer. Dylan nodded and placed a lamp on top of an armchair. "The dump said they'd take anything."

"Oh, really?" I called down to him. "Do they take reject mutants and scientists too?" It was mean, but Jeb and Dylan didn't seem to be *getting* it.

They were not our family.

I grabbed my jacket inside and jumped out the front door, over the canyon.

41

GAZZY WAS HOLDING HIS BREATH, cheeks puffed out, belly pushed out, arms at his sides.

"Puffer fish!" Angel guessed. Gazzy shook his head.

"Blister!" said Iggy, poking Gazzy's cheeks. Gazzy shook his head.

"Knish?" suggested Total. Gazzy shook his head.

"We give up!" Nudge said. "What are you?"

Gazzy let his breath out in a rush. "A grain of rice, cooking!" he said. "*Obviously!* I started off all skinny, then got bigger and bigger!"

Dylan laughed. "Good one," he said. "Never would have guessed—"

A high-pitched whistling noise interrupted him and

filled the room. Just as everyone was registering the smoking ball on the floor, it exploded.

The explosion was small—a flash of blinding light, followed by a sickening stream of pink smoke. Everyone began coughing, practically retching from the noxious smell.

Then, in the next second, there was a huge crunching noise—from above.

"Scatter!" said Gazzy.

They all fanned out around the edges of the room. Angel motioned to Dylan to keep his back against the wall.

"Oh, God, what is that stuff?" Nudge moaned, coughing into her sleeve.

The shock of the gas cloud rendered them useless as the roof above them was ripped apart with loud splintering noises. Then an inhumanly large, hairy hand grabbed some Sheetrock from the ceiling and tore it away with long, ragged yellow claws.

"Oh, my God," Nudge breathed. "Is that an *Eraser?*"

"Everyone, outside!" Angel ordered. It was always better to fight in the air than inside a building, and the smoke felt crippling. But as the flock raced for doors and windows, those doors and windows crashed inward, followed by the hulking, horribly familiar forms of Erasers.

It was like waking up into a nightmare of the past.

"Dinnertime!" one of the Erasers growled, and the others laughed—the same way the flock had heard so many times before. Their wolfish faces were split into ugly yellow-toothed grins, and their small mean eyes glittered with the excitement of the hunt. There were at least ten of them, and they easily weighed more than two hundred pounds each.

The dogs bravely leaped at the wolfmen first. Akila managed to clamp her jaws around one's ankle and draw blood before he kicked her away. Total took to the air, flitting around like a big black mutant moth, snarling and snapping, occasionally getting a bite of Eraser flesh.

It was a good distraction. The kids had a second to catch their breath as the smoke began to dissipate. Then instinct kicked in, and in moments they had launched themselves at their attackers.

"They still smell like garbage!" Gazzy yelled, as the first blows were exchanged. He felt like he might barf.

"Okay, now I'm mad!" Iggy shouted.

Angel glanced over to see a thin trickle of blood coming from his nose.

An Eraser lunged at Angel, and she dodged, screaming bloody murder. She grabbed a floor lamp and connected with the Eraser's heavily boned head, snapping it to one side.

Nearby, Dylan was coughing and gagging from the lingering smoke. And yet he was mercilessly pounding an Eraser, his fists flying almost supernaturally fast. The Eraser was doubled over, unsuccessfully trying to block the blows.

So, the new bird kid had been programmed to fight.

The rest of them were even better trained to fight Erasers, but with the desperate impulse to keep their arms in front of their noses and mouths, they started to lose ground.

One Eraser grabbed Nudge and held her in a death grip even though she screamed and kicked with all her might. A second jumped behind her and grasped her wings brutally.

He was getting ready to break them.

42

THE SUN BEAT DOWN on my shoulders. It felt heavenly to be out flying, my hair streaming back, silence all around. I gazed down at the earth beneath me, the winding streams carved through red canyons, the striated layers of rock revealed by millennia of erosion, my tiny shadow on the ground, barely visible—

And the dark shadow following me, so close, practically right on top of me.

I took a breath, folded my wings down, swung my feet so I was vertical, and snapped my fist up hard. With unerring timing, it connected solidly with a face.

I heard a surprised hiss of breath, felt skin split beneath the force, then dove down, did a somersault in midair, and angled myself to attack from below.

"What the hell is the matter with you!" Fang shouted. One hand was pressed to his face, below his right eye.

"Fang!" I evened myself out till I was flying close to him. Our wings kept us about eight feet apart. "I'm sorry—I didn't know it was you. Why were you sneaking up on me?"

"Who else would it be?" He sounded cranky and kept rubbing his face.

"Anyone! An Eraser, or a Flyboy, or—"

"There aren't any more Erasers," he said, giving me a confused look. "And I don't think there are any more Flyboys either. We haven't seen any in ages. Who else is going to be flying after you except one of us?"

We both thought of Dylan at the same time.

"Sorry," I muttered again. "I just reacted."

His cheek was pink and already swelling—he would have a helluva shiner by tomorrow. "Look, there's a tree over there. Can we stop a minute?"

A huge pine stood at the edge of the tree line on the mountain. We swooped down, slowed, and landed on a large branch.

"Sorry about yesterday," Fang said. He leaned his back against the broad, rough trunk. "I let Dylan get to me. It was stupid. I can't believe I didn't notice the house almost burning down." He gave a brief, wry smile.

"It didn't almost burn down," I said. "Just the couch, really. Gazzy and Ig were making a new stash of detonators, and 'something happened.'"

Fang shook his head and let out a breath, then looked deeply into my eyes. I got that hollow, fluttery feeling again. I wanted to melt into him and forget everything, but something still felt like it had changed.

For some reason, Dylan's face popped into my mind, and it was as though the two of them were side by side: Fang and Dylan. They were night and day. Dylan's face was more open, wanting to talk, to ask questions, to learn. Fang's face was closed, secretive, strong, like the most interesting riddle I would ever find.

"Jeb said the others were complaining about us," I told him. The fresh pine-scented breeze blew my hair around, and I tucked it behind my ear.

"We're all getting used to the...changed dynamics," said Fang. He reached out and took a strand of my hair, immediately getting caught in a tangle. "It's pretty, in the sun," he said, holding the strand out to catch the sun's rays. It was mostly brown but had streaks of dark red and even a little blond.

"Still," I pressed on, "we have to think—"

"No, we don't," Fang whispered, and he tilted his head. I barely had time to breathe in before his warm lips were on mine, for the first time in...days. He put his arms around me and angled his head more.

I was so familiar with him that I could feel how swollen his cheek was, right under his eye. I mean, I knew Fang. I'd always known him. Literally always, my whole life. He'd always been my best friend and my second-in-command.

I didn't really know when our feelings had changed. All I knew was that he was the best thing I had in my life.

He held me closer and closer until we were practically glued together. I don't know how long we stayed there, kissing and murmuring to each other. Finally my stomach rumbled, making us both laugh and break apart, our foreheads still touching.

"I guess I better get to the store," I said, feeling like everything would be all right again in my world. "You coming?"

Fang nodded, and then a low buzzing sound, like a swarm of bees, distracted me. We both looked up through the top of the tree. Very, very high, higher than helicopters usually go, were four black choppers. We could barely see them, barely hear them. Most humans wouldn't have been able to spot them, wouldn't have known they were there.

But they were. And they were headed in the direction of our house.

Without speaking, we let go of the tree and fell outward, then opened our wings as the ground rushed up to meet us.

Time for reality again.

43

DYLAN HADN'T BEEN ALIVE much longer than eight months and didn't know much about flock taboos, but one thing he instinctively knew: *Don't mess with a bird kid's wings.*

And Nudge's were about to be snapped. Then they'd throw her out the window.

"Don't you *dare!*" Dylan cried as he leaped for Nudge. Snarling, an Eraser shot out a boot-clad foot, caught Dylan squarely in the chest, and sent him flying across the room. He slammed into a wall and hit his head hard.

In the midst of the battle, Gazzy raced to the kitchen. One of Iggy's big carving knives, maybe...? A fast glance revealed nothing—the kitchen was cluttered with dirty plates and pots.

He spied a possible weapon, grabbed it, and raced back to the stench-filled living room, where Nudge was still struggling. An Eraser clamped a hairy paw over her mouth, its rough claws scraping her cheek. Gazzy punched a button on his weapon and jabbed it hard into the back of one of Nudge's captors.

"Attack of the Kitchen Appliances!" Gazzy yelped hoarsely, never a great one for stealth.

The mixer blades quickly began to spin, and just as quickly got horribly tangled in the Eraser's long, greasy fur. Gazzy pushed the speed button to "high," and fur actually started to rip out.

The Eraser howled and whirled to kick at Gazzy. The moment he dropped his guard, Nudge twisted away from him hard, and freed one arm. Then she pulled back and gave the other Eraser a huge snap kick right to his stomach.

When he loosened his grip on her, Nudge instantly dropped to the floor and grabbed his ankles, yanking them as hard as she could. In the next moment Akila lunged at him, barking and snarling, and the Eraser couldn't regain his balance. He went tumbling out the window, down, down, down into the canyon below.

Gazzy pushed the mixer into the other Eraser again, ripping out more chunks of fur and skin. The Eraser shrieked in pain, trying to bat the mixer away, but it was hopelessly entangled in his fur.

Iggy's keen sense of smell had been the most assaulted

by the gas bomb and Eraser stench. But the upside was he could easily gauge each Eraser's position. Just as the wounded creature roared at Gazzy, Iggy flung something that glinted in the light as it spun through the air: the blade from his food processor. It sliced through the fur and embedded itself in the Eraser's back.

"Same bat time," said Gazzy, grabbing the Eraser's feet.

"Same bat canyon!" Nudge coughed, helping Gazzy heave the struggling half-man out the window.

That shifted the balance. The flock, Akila, Total, and Dylan could now gang up on the remaining Erasers, two or three on one, and over the next few minutes managed to shove, kick, tip, and otherwise eject every single one of them out the canyon-side windows.

Then it was eerily silent, except for a few wheezes and coughs.

Angel jumped off the deck and flew upward, to see if there were other threats.

"Turn on all the fans!" gasped Dylan, then he leaned over and retched. He'd been breathlessly taking out Erasers since the moment they hit the floor.

Angel came back in, rubbing big dark bruises on her upper arms. "I don't see anything else," she said. "Everyone report." She walked around the room, estimating the damage the way she'd seen Max do.

"Um, this place is shot to hell," said Gazzy.

"Bloody nose," said Iggy. "With red blood."

Now that he'd been able to clear his lungs, Dylan was

examining big gouges in his arm. "I'll be okay, pretty much," he said bravely. "But I'm worried about Nudge."

She was crouched on the floor, twisting awkwardly to look over her shoulder. "I'm not sure, but one of my wings doesn't feel right. Can you sprain a wing?"

"I jammed my pinkie finger," Angel said, frowning. She gritted her teeth, gripped the end of it, and fearlessly yanked it back into alignment.

Akila was panting, and she and Total touched noses. "We're okay," said Total. "But I will never get the taste of Eraser out of my mouth."

Angel held up a hand. "Shh! Incoming!"

Everyone braced as they heard noises outside.

Then Max and Fang landed on the deck, hopping and skipping to avoid all the debris and broken glass. Wide-eyed, Max rushed through the shattered sliding door with Fang close behind her.

"Nice of you to join us," Angel said.

"Gazzy, man, jeezum!" Fang exclaimed. "What the heck have you been *eating,* for God's sake?"

"That was a smoke bomb!" Gazzy defended himself. "Not even I could fill this whole flippin' house!"

44

"WHAT THE HECK HAPPENED?" I asked, taking in Iggy's bloody nose, Nudge's pained face.

"Erasers," said Iggy angrily. "*Erasers* happened. But enough about us. How was your *joyride?*"

"I heard the choppers," I said. "I came back as fast as I could." I was still trying to process the "Erasers" part.

"Whatever, Max." Iggy shook his head angrily. "You and Fang were off together—like always. The rest of us could have died here, but as long as you two get your face time, it doesn't matter!"

"Hey!" came Jeb's voice from outside. "Put down the ladder!" He was just returning from the dump. In a few moments, he was staring at us all in shock. Then he looked with dismay around the living room, which was now a poster child for the benefits of having home insurance. Which, of course, we didn't.

"Erasers attacked," I told him. "Apparently. While I was at the store."

Jeb frowned. "Are you sure they were actual Erasers? Not robots?"

"These were definitely Erasers," Gazzy said. "You can still smell them."

"Look what I found outside." Jeb held up a black duffel bag. "Maybe this'll offer some kind of clue." He opened it, and we all fell silent. Inside were black hoods. Clear vials of liquid. Hypos in cases. There were black plastic body bags.

"Those were for us," said Gazzy, as we gaped at the bag's contents. "They must have been trying to knock us out with that nerve gas stuff."

"Erasers don't use this kind of equipment. Only brute force," Jeb remarked. "Someone else must have been out there too."

"But weren't all the Erasers wiped out?" I asked Jeb. Of anyone, Jeb would be in the know about the wolfboys.

Jeb nodded slowly. "The entire original production line, as well as the next four generations, were all...retired," he said. "But I wonder. After the School closed, the scientists, what was left of them, scattered. It's possible—even likely—that one or more of them have set up shop somewhere else."

"Where are the Erasers now? Do you know?" Fang asked the kids.

"Dumped 'em in the canyon," Angel said, rubbing her hand.

"Good job, guys," I said. "That was the way to go." I tried a grin. "But I bet we'll be smelling them for days, until the vultures finish them off."

Fang strode back out to the deck, hopped up on the railing, and jumped off to investigate the remains. I saw envy and admiration war on Dylan's face.

"So, Dylan, your first Eraser fight," I commented, wondering how he had done.

"He did great," said Total. "He's a machine. Dylan's like the top-of-the-line Cuisinart to Gazzy's hand mixer." Total was a bit of a gourmet, and his point was all but lost on me.

Dylan shrugged as if he'd done nothing at all, even though one arm had ugly gashes on it. His long-sleeved plaid shirt was in tatters.

"Um, we should probably be treating those wounds," I said, sounding a little more concerned than I wanted to. That mother hen thing is a hard habit to break.

"Don't worry, Max. I'll be fine," he said, taking his shirt off so he could check out the damage. I tried to avert my eyes from his muscular torso. But even more distracting was seeing just how shredded his arm really was under that shirt.

"Jeepers!" I couldn't understand how Dylan could be so unflinching with that kind of damage. "Jeb, make yourself useful for once! You've got a medical background, don't you?"

"I think I can fix it, Max," Dylan said, as he pulled together ragged bits of skin and held them firmly in place.

The flock heals faster than normal humans, but what Dylan did next I'd never seen another bird kid even attempt: He raised his wounded arm to his mouth and used his own spit to wet the damaged areas. WTH?

"Eew!" Nudge said, and turned away. I, however, was fascinated. And terrified.

"Just a little trick Dr. Gunther-Hagen taught me," Dylan said, as we watched his skin scab up and heal right before our very eyes.

45

I DIDN'T HAVE TIME to grill Dylan about just how much he'd been subjected to Dr. G.'s experimentation before Fang landed lightly on the deck and came in.

"There's nothing down there," he reported.

"What?" Nudge sounded stunned.

"Some blood. Bits of fur. Iggy's mixer," Fang clarified. "No bodies."

"Whoever sent them picked them up," Total said. "Like trash."

"About my mixer," Iggy began.

"It was all I could find!" Gazzy said.

"You mixed someone to death?" I asked.

"I adapted to the circumstances," Gazzy said, crossing his arms over his chest.

"Hmm," I said, starting to pace. "So—the Erasers are back. And someone came to get them. We didn't hear or see how they got here. Choppers may or may not be related." I rubbed my chin as I walked, trying to put this together.

"It's nice of you to care *now*," Iggy said, stopping me in my tracks.

"What's *that* supposed to mean?" I put my hands on my hips.

"I'll go ahead and name the elephant in the room," Iggy went on, glaring over my shoulder. "You and Fang weren't here when we needed you. You were out there"—he gestured to a wall—"because, let's face it, you guys care about each other now more than you care about the rest of us."

"What? That's crazy! It was just chance. It could have been me and Nudge, or Fang and you. Us not being here didn't make this happen!"

"Unless someone was watching and saw our two best fighters leave," Angel said.

It was a horrible thought, and it hit me right in the gut. My brain whirred.

"Look, I guess it's natural," said Iggy. "You're teenagers, it's springtime, everyone's thoughts are turning to birds and bees and caterpillars and moths..."

"Caterpillars?" Nudge's nose wrinkled.

"No one's thinking about moths," Fang said. I heard anger in his voice.

"It's true," Angel said. "You guys care more about each

other than you do about any of us. And we've just seen how dangerous that is—for *us*."

I was so horrified I couldn't think of a snappy comeback.

"It's time, Max," Angel went on firmly. "You know it is." She looked at the rest of the flock. "You guys know it too. It's time for Max and Fang to move on."

46

"MOVE ON?" I tried to ignore the squeak in my voice. "Have you been breathing next to Gazzy too long? What the heck are you talking about?"

"We used to be one flock," Angel said, steely-eyed. "Now it's like we're a flock of four and a sub-flock of two. So maybe you guys should go be your own flock, by yourselves."

"Listen, missy," I began, letting danger drip from my words. "I'm still here, day in, day out, doing for this flock. So don't be telling me—"

"I don't have to tell you or anyone else anything!" Angel exploded. "We have eyes! We *see* how it is! All you think about is how to get away with Fang for a while! So I think it's time you really got away!"

"I planned the whole birthday party!" I said. "For all of us! I helped create this house! For all of us!"

I shot looks at the rest of the angry—and in a few cases alarmed—flock. Dylan was frowning slightly, his face guarded. I wondered if he'd had anything to do with this.

"Angel?" said Jeb. "Be careful. I agree there might be need for a change. But maybe if I come back, we can all work toge—"

"Max." Angel interrupted Jeb as if he didn't exist. Her voice was quiet and calm. "I love you. I don't wish you harm. But like you've said yourself, we're only as strong as the weakest one of us. Right now, you're making the flock weaker because your head and your heart aren't with us. It's time for you to move on. It's time for me to be the leader."

"You?" Jeb looked confused. I guessed he'd missed the first eighteen times Angel had tried to take over the flock.

"Oh, not this again!" I burst out, waving my arms. "Just once I'd like to be able to turn around without you stabbing me in the back!"

Angel's face paled, but she stood firm. "Max, this has been coming for some time. You're trying to have it all, and you just can't. Look—it's time for a vote. Max goes. Everyone who agrees, raise your hand."

I blustered some more, but my heart sank as Iggy slowly raised his hand. His nose had stopped bleeding, but dark bruises were forming around his eyes.

Nudge, my Nudge, was next. Her cheeks were scraped,

her shirt collar flecked with blood. She looked near tears, like she was making an impossible choice—but still choosing not me.

Gazzy raised his hand, not looking at me. His knuckles were swollen and scratched. And of course Angel had her hand up.

"Fang?" I turned to him. He wasn't looking at me. He was glowering at Dylan, who was ever-so-subtly shaking his head. Like they were having some private guy talk.

"Fang! Tell them they're overreacting."

"Everyone is overreacting," Fang said very slowly. "Even you."

For a moment, I was speechless. Was Fang turning his back on me? Did Dylan have mind control powers like Angel? Was he doing a number on Fang?

Anything seemed possible.

"You're my family," I began, then stopped quickly as my voice threatened to break. I cleared my throat and tried again. "After the last time the flock split up, I swore I would do anything to keep us together, no matter what, for always. But it kind of takes *all* of us *wanting* to stay together." I let out my breath slowly, to keep from crying. I shook my head. "I think you guys are making a mistake."

The room was completely still and silent.

"But I can't make you want me to stay." I blinked a couple times, as if I would suddenly wake from an awful dream into a better reality—like, some stranger coming at me with an ice pick, ready to gouge my eyes out.

"So you're sure? You want me to go?"

Nudge's lip was quivering; none of them seemed happy, but they didn't seem to be changing their minds either.

I couldn't look at Fang. If he'd been holding up his hand, I would have wanted to just drop into the canyon like a stone, wings tucked in tight.

I nodded and swallowed. "Okay, then. Later."

I turned and sprinted out through the smashed deck doors, bounced once off the deck railing, and launched myself into the sky, which seemed a million times bigger and wilder than it ever had.

BOOK THREE

WHAT HAPPENS IN HOLLYWOOD... STAYS IN HOLLYWOOD

47

I FELT PRACTICALLY BLINDED by pain and shock and had so many tears streaming from my eyes that I could barely see where I was flying.

I opened my mouth and shrieked, as loud and as wildly as I wanted. "Ohhgodohhnooooiiihitjusthurrrtsss-sooomuuuch!" The scream was torn from my throat by the wind, and finally I choked, sucking in air, half sobbing, my voice raw from yelling for so long.

In overdrive, I can hit speeds of close to three hundred miles per hour, and so in less than half an hour I'd gone into the next state over. Now Utah stared back at me blankly as I slowed and came to a drifting stop at the top of a tree. I had to take a minute out of my new life to...break down and sob like a baby. I worked my way steadily through rage, hurt, embarrassment, back through rage, and then to some random emotion that seemed to need ice cream.

Gulping, I saw a heart-stoppingly familiar black streak in the sky, headed right for me. Was he coming just to say good-bye?

I desperately prayed that he hadn't heard any of my meltdown. The whole thing was such a huge slobbery mess that I couldn't take one more iota of emotion.

"Hey," I said hoarsely, as he landed on a neighboring branch, making the tree sway. I wiped my face quickly, knowing I had to look like hell, my eyes bleary from freeze-dried tears.

"Fancy meeting you here," he said, with his funny lopsided smile, and I almost burst into tears again.

My eyes must have been full of questions, because he shrugged and said, "Things seem somewhat under control. Jeb wants to take over the flock again. I figured I'd let him and Angel duke it out."

I'm supposed to be brave, right? Prove it, Max. I forced myself to ask: "Are you, um, going back?"

"Nah," he said, brushing hair out of my face. "Figured I'd rather hang with you."

I felt hope light my face, and I didn't try to hide it.

"You know how I feel," said Fang, and he bent down, holding on to his branch, and kissed me. I felt like we were suspended in air, and having Fang here, knowing that he, at least, had chosen me, everything seemed a smidgen less agonizingly painful.

"So what should we do now?" I asked breathlessly when we broke away from each other. I'd been the leader so long—I was always the one who decided where we were going, what we were going to do. It felt freeing to be asking *him* to decide.

"Actually, I'm thinking...Vegas," he said. "Let's go to Las Vegas."

"Las Vegas?" I repeated stupidly.

"Yeah," he said, trailing one finger down my cheek. I felt a coolness there, as if he'd hit a stray tear. "I figure—not too far away, full of freaks so we'll blend, plenty of weird stuff to do..."

I smiled and breathed easier for the first time in hours. "Sounds perfect."

48

"HAVE YOU BACKED UP the data?" The head of information finished scanning the shift tech's notes for Area 8 and leaned over her shoulder to look at her computer screen. "Subject Twenty-two appears to be...abnormal. Off program. Let's take a closer look at the images."

The tech clicked her mouse quickly through the static scenes. The image on the screen changed from an empty living area with one lamp burning to a darkened kitchen area. The kitchen was a mess, with dirty plates and pots and glasses stacked on every surface. Food containers had been left open, unrefrigerated. The next image was a long, empty hallway with large windows on one side. After that was a bedroom.

"This is Subject Twenty-two, sleeping in Subject One's

bed, since she isn't there," the tech said. "During the day he's mostly been practicing flying, but at night he's been restless, not sleeping deeply. It could be that his circadian rhythms haven't stabilized yet. His physio readings suggest that he's anxious or unhappy."

"Yes. His prime focus went away."

"I see. Before he went to sleep, he walked around the room, examining everything, touching everything, even smelling things."

"He's imprinting," said the head of information. "That's good. But the notes indicate he's made no attempt to follow Subject One. Can you confirm?"

"His flying skills are improving, but at this stage wouldn't enable long-distance—"

"Irrelevant," the head jumped in dismissively. "His programming should compel him to use any means available. Possibly a minor malfunction," she speculated, dropping the tech's notes on the desk. "But possibly a major one. Keep an especially close eye on that one's stats." She swiveled on her heel and in a flash was gone.

The tech bit her lip. The heads—as intimately familiar with the details of their constructions as they were—somehow all seemed to forget that the subjects were not, in fact, robots.

There was no malfunction. It was simply that the soul could not be programmed.

49

I WAS WORKING through Italian spumoni on a cone as Fang and I threaded our way amid the streaming crowds on the sidewalk. Those of you who haven't been to Vegas—well, it's bizarre in sort of a "let's gussy up this car wreck" kind of way. It's Disney World meets the seedy underbelly of America. But with more liquor and people smoking. A grown-up amusement park.

"I'm dying to go to a casino," I confessed to Fang.

"We'll have to throw ourselves three more birthday parties first," he said. "It's illegal—we're underage."

"So when has that ever stopped us?" I stared at him. "That's just a way to make sure crazy kids don't spend all their parents' money. We're not crazy, and we don't have any parents' money. Just our own hard-earned cash from all those CSM air shows we did."

"Which has gotta be running low about now. You really want to risk losing it?"

"Don't get all grown-up on me. This is, like, our *vacation* from being the grown-ups of the flock. And I want to go...." I looked around at the spectacularly campy scenery.

"There," Fang declared, pointing to a building in the shape of a...horse? It definitely topped the Bizarre-o-Meter of novelty architecture. "The Trojan Horse."

Suddenly I was having second thoughts. "Wasn't that, like, a giant sculpture that was full of enemy soldiers or something? Back in the old days?"

Fang looked blank. "Guess I missed that lesson in Max's Home School." He took my hand. "Come on!"

We strolled in easily across the dizzyingly patterned carpet. Barbie doll women with trays of drinks were zipping around helping to get people loopy so they'd spend more money. Even without a drop of alcohol, it took about two seconds for me to become seized with a very unnatural need to gamble.

Fang leaned close and whispered, "Don't freak out, but there are cameras in the ceiling every couple feet." Ordinarily, that fact would guarantee I'd break out in paranoid hives. "And notice the guys in dark suits standing around watching everyone? Don't worry. They're just looking for cheaters."

"Cheaters? Us?" I smiled. "I guess we're safe."

The flock had always looked a little older than our biological ages—guess that came from being evolutionary wonders. But I was surprised that people didn't boot us out immediately. Imagine *money* being more important than *law enforcement!*

We got a bunch of quarters and parked ourselves in front of a Treasure Island slot machine. I fed a quarter into the slot and pulled the arm. The wheels spun fast, eventually stopping with cherries, a weight, and the number seven.

My eyes narrowed and I pushed another quarter in.

Another miss.

"That machine took my money!" I said. "I must have revenge! Fang, get on that machine next to me," I ordered, spilling half of my quarters into a separate plastic bucket for him. "This could take a while."

And so our hypnotic rally began. Seriously, those spinning wheels can really send you into the zone. I guess that's the point.

Maybe that explains why it only took about fifteen minutes for the machine to start messing with me.

'Cause instead of cherries, bars, and numbers, I saw a cartoony wolf face pop up.

Then another.

Then another.

Jackpot?

"Jackpot, Max!" I heard the voice of Dr. Gunther-Hagen come from behind me.

50

I WHIRLED AROUND and saw no one. No psychotic mad scientists, anyway.

"Jackpot, Max! Jackpot!" It was Fang, and he was giggling hysterically.

For those of you just joining us, Fang doesn't giggle. Especially *hysterically*.

So for a second, this seemed like one of the weirder dreams of recent days, until Fang clutched my shoulders and started shaking me. "Check it out, Max!"

The jangling sound of metal coins rushing out of Fang's machine suddenly entered my consciousness. Fang had morphed into a wide-eyed maniac scrambling to scoop all of the change into his cup, then mine. "Get another cup!" he ordered, and I grabbed two more that had been orphaned nearby.

While Fang focused on the money, I did a 360 and started to sweat. Downside of a jackpot? People notice you. And in our case, it wasn't all pat-on-the-back, "Oh, congratulations! How wonderful for you!" More like "Who the hell are you and could you even *possibly* be eighteen years old?"

As I saw figures moving toward us, I had a vision of troops inside the Trojan Horse flattening their enemy as they swarmed out. "Outta here *now,* Fang!" I said in my most don't-even-think-of-arguing-with-me voice.

Clutching four heaping cups of coins, we booked it into a glass elevator that delivered us gamblin' fools down, down, down the leg of the Trojan Horse to ground level.

"Remind me never to go to a place called the Trojan Horse again," I said.

"What're you talking about? It was good luck," Fang countered.

"Not exactly," I said, as the glass door slid open and Dr. Hoonie-Goonie was standing there to greet us.

51

DID I WHIRL INSTANTLY, fists clenched, legs tensing for battle? Or did I stay calm, act casual, and walk right on by the doc as if I hadn't even seen him?

You guessed it—neither. Instead, I dropped one of my cups of coins. Easily a couple hundred dollars. Fang seemed more upset by the spillage than by the looming threat of evil.

"Hello, Max, Fang," said Dr. Gunther-Hagen, smiling as he watched Fang scramble to recover his winnings. "Strange seeing you here. I didn't think you were the gambling types."

"We're not," I said. "Fang, leave that money for some poor soul who really needs it," I said, all Mother Teresa again. Except I didn't leave my cups of cash behind.

I stepped out of the elevator, squinting in the bright light. "Why are you here?" See, this is where my lack of social graces comes in handy. I don't waste time and energy on thinking of what the nice thing to do is.

Dr. Hans's eyebrows rose. "I'm here for a professional convention, being held at one of the resorts. But why are you here? Where's the rest of the flock?"

"At Ripley's," I said. "So, what, you saw us and decided to just pop in, say hi?"

"Yes," said Dr. Hans pleasantly. "Is Dylan with you? How is he progressing?"

"Dandy!" I lied again. "We left him over at one of the craps tables. That way." I pointed back to the elevator. "I'm sure he can't wait to see you!"

"We have to go," said Fang, putting his hand on my arm.

"Wait, please," said Dr. Hans. "I'm happy to have run into you. I wanted to reiterate what I said in Africa. And I wanted to make sure you received my offer for Iggy. Is it not compelling? You could give him the gift of sight, in return for a little cooperation. You could be invaluable to my project because—well, you're a miracle, really."

Gosh, a miracle! It had been ages since someone called me that. Actually, no one had ever called me that.

"You planning to turn Max into another one of your *mistakes*?" Fang asked, his face cold and still.

Dr. G-H looked around, as if realizing what a public

place this was. He gestured us over toward some isolated benches in the entry plaza. "The apocalypse is coming. You've been on a mission to save the world. Do you understand how you're supposed to do that?"

Okay, the details on that had been sketchy, but I wasn't about to admit it.

"By having you chop off one of my wings to see if it grows back? I don't think so."

He went on. "Max, I promise you will remain intact. My research will help current humans adapt, so they can live in the radically different environment we'll all be facing. We estimate that more than half the world's population will simply disappear; I've found a way to keep some people alive long enough to ensure that the human race isn't extinguished entirely." His voice was pleading, his face earnest.

"You're a prince," I said. "But I gave you my answer back in Africa."

He paused a second, then continued. "I anticipate people will be scared and worried. Most of them won't understand what I hope to accomplish. But if you were my spokesperson, demonstrating that being different can be wonderful and even necessary, then I could get many, many more people to understand and accept my program."

Who did this guy think he was? The world's savior? Was that position even open? And what did he want me to be? A walking, talking, flying commercial?

"It seems like a worthy cause," I said. I felt Fang's muscles tense. "Tell you what—I'll go ahead and jump on this crazy bandwagon. Count me in."

Dr. Hans's eyes widened and a smile lit his face. "Max, that's wonderf—"

"My price is a million dollars." I know. I'm bad.

"My dear"—he glanced with amusement at my and Fang's hoard of coins—"I do believe you just said you didn't need any money."

"I said we weren't *gambling* types. I'm all about serious business, Doc. And I'm telling you that a million dollars is what it will take for me to even consider this gig."

I could see the wheels turning in his head. I bet those hamsters were tired.

"I could do a million dollars," he said slowly, nodding.

Oh, I forgot—the guy was a billionaire arts patron and he owned a bunch of huge pharma companies that bank-rolled all his plans.

"I meant a million dollars a *day*," I revised. Don't ever say I'm not a tough negotiator.

"This isn't a joke, Max," he said coldly. "You might think carefully about what you say to me. You've already lied to me once today. I know the flock isn't with you. I also know Dylan isn't either, even though he *should* be." I felt Fang flinch next to me. "You consistently ignore my advice, and you *will* regret it if you continue to do so. I have great resources at my disposal. I can help you tremendously, and I want to. I can also do the opposite of that."

I stood my ground. "You evil scientists are all the same—evil. Count me out."

Fang and I brushed past Dr. God and walked quickly but smoothly to the exit. It was barely noon, and I'd already made a huge enemy.

Dang, I'm good.

52

"OKAY, TRY THIS ONE," Gazzy said, handing a hot rod magazine to Iggy. Gazzy guided his finger to touch the photograph on the page.

"Mostly red, I can feel that part—but let me try without touching it." He concentrated. "Hmm, nice. Sort of curvy. But not like a Porsche. Wait...No, it's really low and flat but...not a Lamborghini. How about...Let me cheat a little here...." He touched the picture again. "I'm gonna go out on a limb and say—Bugatti?"

Gazzy jumped up. "No *way!* I can't believe you got that!"

"Hey guys! You've gotta come out here!" Dylan called urgently from the deck.

"What now?" Nudge asked, pulling her earbuds out.

She was in the middle of a *What Not to Wear* download marathon.

"Probably another Eraser attack," Iggy said, sounding bored.

Angel scampered out into the blackness, ready to deliver orders from the deck if necessary.

"Ugh!" Nudge whined. "I wish they'd wait until I finish this episode."

"Seriously, guys," Dylan insisted, but he sounded excited. "The sky is amazing tonight. Check it out!"

"Oh, joy." Iggy scowled, then softened his tone. "Go ahead, Gaz," he said. "All this vision stuff tonight has tired me out."

Minutes later, the flock had peeled themselves away from what they had been doing and were stepping out onto the deck in the cool, clear night. Even Iggy decided to join the crew. Dylan was flat on his back. The deck was only just as wide as he was tall.

"Come down here," he instructed. "It's better this way. You don't have to crane your neck. Can you believe what's going on up there?"

"I don't see much going on," Nudge said. "There's a lot of stars, though."

"Jeb taught us the constellations," Angel said, a little wistfully, after they had all situated themselves. "A long time ago."

"What're they?" Dylan asked blankly.

"Gosh, you *do* need help, don't you?" Gazzy commented. "You should have gone to Max's Home School."

Dylan chuffed. "Yeah. A little late for that."

"Well, for starters, there's the Little Dipper." It was Jeb's voice from inside. He'd appeared behind the screen door quietly. "Can you see it, guys? Do you remember?"

"Yeah. I used to call them the Dipsticks," Gazzy reminisced. "Back when I was a dumb little kid."

"I know Orion!" Nudge bragged. "I see his belt over there at about two o'clock."

"Jeb, can you show us again?" Angel asked, sounding more like her younger, more innocent self. "Like Cassiopeia, Andromeda, Cancer, and stuff?"

"I'm totally confused about what you guys are talking about," Dylan said.

"With you on that, Dyl." Iggy put his feet on the wooden deck rail and his hands behind his head, staring up at nothing.

"Can't you see that meteor?" Dylan asked. "Over there. See? The flame is almost, like, *greenish*.... Whoa! It's getting bigger—man, how can you *not* see that?"

Iggy snickered. "Dude, even *I* know that shooting stars last for like, less than a second."

"Oooh!" Angel cried, just as the flaming tail appeared in the sky, fast as a flash of lightning.

"Nice one!" Nudge cheered. "How'd you know it was coming, Dylan?"

"I could just see it. I don't know how you guys

missed—ooh, there's another one coming! Right over there!" Dylan pointed left with conviction. Everyone was quiet.

Iggy broke the silence. "I can see the International Space Station too," he said.

Seconds later, they all drew in their breaths as another flash exploded in the sky. "Must be a meteor shower," Jeb speculated.

Dylan nodded. "Yep—yeah, I see one—no, two, three more coming! Look!"

Jeb slid the door open and took a step out onto the deck, fascinated.

"One," he counted as they appeared several moments later. "Two, three."

Gazzy gave a low whistle.

"Dylan," Angel asked very quietly. "Can you see the future?"

Dylan paused. "I...I don't know," he answered. "I guess I just see really well." He squinted. "And I hate to say this, Iggy, but...I actually *can* see the International Space Station."

"Cool, man," Iggy said. "Hey, by the way, can you spare one of your superhero eyeballs for me, Dyl?"

Dylan laughed. "All yours, Iggy."

"If you can see so well, Dylan," Angel asked curiously, "why didn't you see those Erasers coming?"

For that, Dylan had no answer.

53

"THERE IS NO WAY those people aren't genetically modified," I said, taking another handful of popcorn. In the other city that never sleeps, we weren't sleeping. In fact, we were at one of the Cirque du Soleils, watching some little Chinese girls fold themselves into knots while spinning plates on their feet and balancing balls on their heads.

"It's completely unnatural," Fang agreed.

"So they're mutants, they're weird, and here they are, holding down jobs. There is hope after all." I ate more popcorn, unable to tear my eyes away from people doing stuff that I just couldn't believe they could do.

We'd just come from the MGM resort, where it had

happened to be Cub Day — they'd had two super-cute lion cubs playing in a huge glassed-in area.

"Now, why couldn't they have put just a smidge of lion DNA into our mix?" I'd asked. "That would be so cool."

Fang had groaned. "That's all we need. Another two percent of something else in our genes. Excellent."

"Still, just a touch of lion — we'd be even stronger, faster," I had said wistfully. "And more graceful."

"You're already strong, fast, and...somewhat graceful, sometimes," Fang had said. "You want *fuzzy ears?*"

I had dropped the subject. But now, looking at act after act of inhumanly flexible and powerful humans, I almost wanted just a little touch of something else.

"I'm thinking those kids have extra vertebrae," I whispered to Fang.

"Be happy with your ninety-eight-two-percent split," he whispered back. "Next thing you know, you'll be grafted with, like, DNA from an *elephant seal.* Or a bear. 'Where's Max? Oh, she's *hibernating,*'" Fang said. I had just taken a sip of soda, and now my graceful self snorted it through my nose.

Max.

"What?" Oh. Voice. '*Ssup?*

Get out of there now.

Without hesitation I got to my feet. Fang looked at me in surprise, saw the expression on my face, and immediately got up too. I did a fast scan and saw guards at each entrance, but they didn't seem to be paying attention to us.

So where...

Max, up!

I crouched down, ready to jump into the air and to take flight at the slightest sign of danger, but in the next second, strong arms grabbed me.

54

"DON'T STRUGGLE," said the guy holding me—the "Russian Superman." He had an act with huge rubber bands attached to his belt. He'd been jumping high and "flying" over the audience off and on all night. Now he pulled me way up to the top of the enormous tent, and the bands tightened so we were hovering there.

The audience below was oohing and aahing at the lucky girl in the audience who got to fly with the Russian Superman. Spotlights were trained on us, and the audience was going crazy.

"Who do you work for?" I growled, gauging my options.

"This is for your own good," he said, which was, in case you're wondering, *the wrong answer.*

Time to blow my cover as Ordinary Teenager. I raised one knee high, then smashed my foot backward as hard as I could, connecting with his kneecap, hearing it snap. The Russian Superman stifled a shriek, and his hold on me lessened just slightly.

Slightly was enough. I jerked my arms out sideways, and his fingers scrabbled to keep me, without success. I started to drop, and people in the audience started to scream, waiting for the poor girl to go splat in the center ring.

But of course it took only a second for me to pop out my wings, pushing downward hard so that I rose up before I'd even gotten close to the ground.

Now the audience was really going wild—shouting, clapping, whistling at the Amazing Winged Girl from the Cirque du Soleil.

The Amazing Winged Girl needed a way out. The Russian Superman, holding his knee, was staring at me in shock. I tried to shade my eyes to see Fang, then another huge burst of excitement came from the crowd, and I saw him flying up to me, outlined in the spotlights.

We can't hover, so to stay aloft we have to move forward. I made small circles near the top of the tent, searching for an escape route, trying to stay away from the backstage crew up in the metal catwalks high above the ground.

Fang swooped low, making people scream, then swooped back up again. He passed me, showed me the switchblade he'd pulled from his cargo pocket, and headed toward a tent wall.

I was zigzagging as I saw Fang grab a rope against the wall, hang on, and slice through the heavy plasticized nylon of the tent.

There was tremendous applause—we were a very popular act. Then an all-too-familiar sound hissed past my ear, and I dropped fast, swung around, and raced over to Fang.

"They're shooting—they've got silencers," I reported urgently just as he sliced an X large enough for us to slip through. Another bullet pinged off a nearby catwalk, and Fang folded his wings and slipped out of the tent.

I took one quick glance down as I started to edge through the hole, and a roaming spotlight picked him out of the crowd. Dr. Scary. Here at the Cirque du Soleil, where we were under attack.

What a coinkydink.

55

"WILL IT HURT?" Nudge asked quietly as she put on her shoes. Early-morning light was breaking through the leafy trees outside and sprinkling sun across the room, and the flock was gathering for their next "field trip."

"Oh, I'm sure not," Angel said vaguely, digging around in her backpack for her coupon. "I mean, not more than, like, getting punched by an Eraser. Or a sprained wing."

"Comforting," Iggy commented. "I think it's a great idea, personally, but I don't think Gazzy's so thrilled." Iggy went to look for the Gasman as the others headed toward the front door.

"Are you sure everyone wants to go through this, Angel?" Dylan asked. "I mean, most of us aren't...fond of needles. Lab associations and all."

"Come on, guys. If Max were here, you'd be all into this," Angel said a little testily. "The tattoos were Max's birthday presents to us, after all."

"Not to me," Dylan said, wistful.

Just then, Jeb strode in, looking like he'd just rolled out of bed. "Good lord, Angel! What did I just hear you talking about?"

"We're going to get our tattoos. Max gave us gift certificates for our birthdays."

"You most certainly are not!" Jeb said firmly, just like the old days. "You're underage—it's illegal. I won't hear of it."

"You're not the leader, Jeb," Angel reminded him. "I am."

"Well, Jeb's a grown-up," Nudge pointed out.

Angel's eyes narrowed. "You guys elected *me* leader."

"Hmm," said Nudge, sounding doubtful. "More like we elected Max *not* leader. I wonder what she's doing?"

"You mean besides not worrying about us?" Angel started to feel angry. "I'll tell you what she's doing—she and Fang are off somewhere, having a great time, not even thinking about us! They're all cozy, just the two of them, and've probably forgotten our names by now!"

"I bet not," Nudge said stubbornly, as Iggy and Gazzy entered the room.

"Look, everyone, I have news for you," Jeb said. "In the future, it might be that each one of you has a flock of his or her own to lead."

Everyone looked around, blinking in surprise. Jeb sat

down on the floor and motioned for them to do the same. He had a lot of explaining to do.

"Max has actually been a pretty good leader—she's kept you alive; she's taught you how to survive. I know you have your problems with her. I do too." He gave a little laugh. "But here you are: You're a flock and you need a leader. Angel says that she's the leader, and I guess you guys are agreeing to it. So here are my questions:

"What are you going to do differently from Max? How will it be an improvement? How will you handle another attack like the one yesterday? How will you all work together to grow and change and adapt, to maximize your chances of survival?"

Angel thought. She listened to her Voice. She thought some more.

"Jeb? I've been thinking about it and I have something to say to you. To everyone." She paused. One by one they stopped what they were doing and looked at her. "Maybe *living* is more important than just *surviving*."

56

"THIS IS IT, SIR." The lead geologist double-checked her GPS and overlaid its image with a satellite-based graph. "Satellite and radar confirm it. This stream leads to the underground source that the subjects get their water from."

"I hope you're right," Dr. Gunther-Hagen said icily. He was irritated at the Cirque du Soleil blunder, tired from the late-hour flight, and altogether eager for some progress in this project. "Your performance up till now has been pathetic. Be glad I'm *somewhat* more forgiving than Mr. Chu."

The geologist swallowed and rechecked her instruments with fingers that trembled slightly. "No, this is it," she said, trying to make her voice strong. "I'm positive."

"Okay, then," said Dr. Gunther-Hagen. "Release the reactant."

Another agent opened a foam cooler. A fog of dry ice swirled around them like early-morning mist. He carefully pulled on heavy gloves that protected him from fingertip to elbow. Following that, a gas mask covered his face. The others moved away to stand upwind. The agent carefully removed a test tube from the dry ice with tongs. He uncapped it, and after a moment's hesitation, tipped the test tube so its pale pink liquid flowed into the thin mountain stream.

"Of course, this will affect everything it comes into contact with," he murmured, praying that Dr. Gunther-Hagen knew what he was doing.

"Not necessarily," said Dr. Gunther-Hagen. "It's been specialized to bind only to certain receptors. These mutants have them; not many other species do."

The team was silent as the reactant blended invisibly with the crystal-clear stream. Within thirty minutes, it would infiltrate the natural water reservoir that served the flock's house.

Dr. Gunther-Hagen could barely contain his excitement. Now the real experiments would start.

57

ALL EYES WERE ON ANGEL. She was almost vibrating with anticipation. Max would never have been able to do this in a million years. Max never would have *wanted* to. In fact, she would have threatened to lock them all in their rooms if someone suggested it.

Now she tapped a pencil against the tabletop. "Attention! Everybody, listen up! I've called you all here to make my announcement!" she said. "Get ready, because I have a huge surprise!"

"Do we need any more surprises?" Iggy asked.

"I'm the leader of this flock," she announced, "and I want to announce some improvements we're going to make."

"What kind of improvements?" Iggy asked, leaning on his broom.

"Well, first, I'm abolishing bedtime," Angel said, nodding firmly.

"We didn't have much of a bedtime before," Nudge pointed out.

Angel frowned at her. "I mean, if we want to sleep all day and stay up all night, then that's what we'll do!"

Gazzy shrugged. "Okay."

"No more homeschooling!" Angel said.

"Hear, hear," said Iggy, clapping.

"I'm still going to learn stuff," Nudge said. "I'm halfway through the Rosetta Stone level one for French."

"If you want to, that's fine," said Angel graciously. "But right now, I'm going to announce our best, most exciting project ever!"

"We're going to buy our own car?" Gazzy asked with raised eyebrows.

"Have parties every week?" Nudge guessed.

"How about a little order, a little taking care of business?" Total muttered as he trotted into the room. "That *would* be a huge surprise."

Angel ignored him. Even though she was the one who had rescued him from the lab back in New York, secretly she wondered if he was more on Max's side now. "Okay, everyone, saddle up!" She beamed at them. "We have a long flight ahead of us!"

"To where?" Nudge asked.

"A concert!" Angel said. "In Hollywood! Where we've signed up to appear as special celebrity guests!"

Blank faces looked back at her.

"Is this a joke?" Iggy finally asked.

"No! It's going to be so fabulous!" Angel said. "The concert is a benefit, for fixing up a section of Santa Monica Boulevard. All kinds of famous people are part of it, and they want us to help. If they advertise that the flock will be there, thousands more people will come!"

"And a percentage of them will be toting semiautomatic handguns, or weird mind-control chips, or heck, even bows and arrows!" said Iggy. "There's a reason we don't go out in public much."

"Is this a CSM benefit?" Nudge asked. "I mean, Santa Monica Boulevard?"

"No," said Angel. "But it's totally cool. I've talked to our agents—"

"What agents?" Nudge interrupted.

"The ones I've been interviewing," said Angel smugly. "The ones who offered us the best deal. They're going to pay us a whole bunch of money, and guarantee our safety too. We're supposed to call them when we get to the Villa d'Arbanville."

"Villa d'Arbanville? I've heard of that place," said Nudge. "That's where stars hang out! The lobby was voted 'the best place to break up' by *Superstar* magazine!"

Finally, Dylan spoke up. "Sounds like fun, but...I think I'll be staying here."

All eyes turned to him in surprise. "C'mon, man—live a little," Iggy said. He was just starting to get used to having Dylan around.

"Not sure I have time for partying." He didn't look anyone in the eye. "I've got to keep working on my flying," he explained. It wasn't a very good excuse, but Angel could work with it.

"Well, then you're coming with us, Dylan," she announced, feeling decisive and leaderly. "We're gonna fly eight hundred miles to get there. Practice makes perfect." Angel tried to zero her powers of influence in on Dylan. She wouldn't take no for an answer.

"I'll see if I can hitch a ride on a private jet," said Jeb. "Total, you and Akila are welcome to come with me. Dylan, you can come with us too," said Jeb.

Dylan shook his head, making some of his shaggy, sun-streaked hair fall into his turquoise eyes. "No. I'll fly with the others," he said determinedly, but he seemed sad.

Angel saw the intent look in his eyes. And for the first time, she picked up on some of his thoughts.

He had been hoping Max would come home.

58

"THIS IS THE COOLEST HOTEL EVER!" squealed Nudge, flopping facedown onto a king-size bed.

Angel was trying to get the snarls out of her blond curls, still wet from her shower. Through the doorway to the room next door, she heard Gazzy ordering room service—again. The kitchen had probably had to send someone out to get more groceries.

Nudge rolled off the bed and looked at herself in the mirror. "I'm twelve now. I don't look different, but I feel different." She stretched her wings out slowly, their feathers shades of tan, caramel, and coffee.

"You do look different," said Angel. "We're all taller. You don't look like a little kid anymore—more teenagery. Iggy and...the others have really started looking older."

"Can I come in?" Dylan leaned in the doorway connecting their two rooms.

"Sure," said Nudge. "Have you recovered? That was a long flight."

"I can't believe I didn't drop like a rock over the Grand Canyon," Dylan said, leaning against the dresser. "I bet I won't be able to move my wings tomorrow."

"You did great," said Angel. "Aren't you glad you came with us?"

Dylan shrugged and brushed some hair out of his face. He already looked like a Hollywood star—some teenage girls had whispered and pointed at him when the flock had been checking in.

Dylan was doing pretty well at fitting in with the rest of the flock. He wasn't demanding, and he was a good listener and a good fighter. Angel loved Fang a lot, but Dylan was…easier. Warmer. He talked more. It was almost as if he were made to be with them.

A knock on the door made Nudge pull her wings in fast.

Angel hurried over and peeped through the eyehole.

"Bad guys or good guys?" Nudge asked.

Angel smirked. "Bad guys," she said, and pulled open the door.

Four men came in, looking around with avid curiosity. They were all very tan, dressed casually but in nice clothes and jackets. One of them was chewing gum.

"Who are you?" Dylan asked.

"Joe Harkins," one of them said, holding out a tanned hand. "Pleased to meetcha. From Talent Unlimited. Here's my card." He pressed a business card into Dylan's hand.

Another knock on the door almost went unheard as the men started shaking each bird kid's hand, introducing themselves eagerly. Gazzy opened the door and let in Jeb, Total, and Akila.

"Whoa, you brought your dogs!" one man exclaimed, and Angel hoped Total wouldn't bite him on the ankle.

"Hello, son," one of the men said to Dylan, looking him up and down. "Now, that's what I call star quality! All of you, of course! Talent Unlimited couldn't be happier to offer representation!"

"Talent Unlimited?" Jeb asked.

"Yep! And your kids here are pure gold," said Joe Harkins. He literally rubbed his hands together. "Now, let's talk numbers. Kids, why don't you guys go play in the pool downstairs while Dad and I talk business?"

Angel heard Total choking back laughter. It was time to show these guys who was the leader.

"He's not our dad," she said, her face serious. "He won't be making decisions for us." Keeping her eyes on the agents, she unfolded her wings.

The men stared. Angel could almost see dollar signs in their eyes, like in cartoons.

"I'll be negotiating our contract," Angel said solemnly. "Why don't we sit down over here?"

The room fell silent as the men waited for someone to

say she was kidding. When no one did, Angel motioned again to the table and chairs set up in the suite's dining area. The men hesitated.

"I hear the usual agent share is fifteen percent," Angel said, concentrating, focusing. "We need ninety-five percent."

Chuckling at Angel's joke, they relaxed and trickled over to the table to sit down.

Of course, Angel wasn't joking. An hour later, they got up, looking pale, shaken, and incredulous. They stared at the copies of the contract on the table like they couldn't believe they had actually signed them.

"'Kthnxbye!" Angel said brightly, opening the door for them. The men wandered out as if they had just barely survived a crash.

"What did you do to them?" Jeb asked.

"Persuaded them." Angel's too innocent face wouldn't have fooled a kindergartner. "Isn't that what a good leader would do?"

"Angel, we've talked about—," Jeb began.

"Come on, everyone!" Angel cried. "Press conference by the pool!"

59

"REPORTERS?" GAZZY ASKED. "Max will kill us if she finds out about this."

"Max isn't in charge anymore," Angel reminded him coolly. "It's time the world knew about our special abilities."

"I'm not feeling that special right now," said Iggy, hunched over in a chair. "I've been feeling weird all afternoon."

Nudge frowned. "Me too. Not sick, exactly, but weird. Like, tingly, all over."

Jeb heard this last bit and he quickly searched Nudge's face. "Tingly? On your skin or inside?"

"All over," said Nudge.

"I feel that way too," said Gazzy. "I didn't even realize it till you said it. I thought it was just the PowerDrives kicking in."

"Let's get through this press conference," Angel said briskly, "then we can figure out what's going on." She was feeling weird herself, but it was showtime, folks.

Ten minutes later, they were stretched out on lounge chairs by the hotel pool.

"Where's our waiter?" Nudge asked ten minutes after that. She tipped her pink star-shaped sunglasses down on her nose. "I need more iced tea."

Dylan stood up. "I was going to get some — I'll get yours too."

"Here are the reporters," Angel announced, pointing at a small throng of people who were being let into the fenced pool area. The private security team frisked each one and checked their names off on a list.

Dylan reappeared with the iced teas, and several of the reporters gasped or went speechless at the sight of him. Angel grinned. Who needed Fang when they had Dylan? The flock was a whole lot nicer to look at — and be a part of — with him around.

She motioned for the security people to let the reporters come closer. There were about ten of them, some carrying microphones, some with big video cameras on their shoulders.

"Hi!" she said, putting on a party face. "Thanks for coming! We can answer questions for ten minutes, and then there will be a photo op. Who's first?"

"Where are your parents?" cried one reporter. "Do they have wings?"

"Our parents were a test tube and a turkey baster," Angel said. "No wings."

"Can you actually fly, or has that been a publicity stunt?" called another reporter.

In response, Gazzy shook out his wings, climbed onto the diving board, bounced a couple times, then launched himself into the air. There were gasps and murmurs of excitement as he moved up and down with each flap of his wings, eating an ice cream cone. Then he popped the last of the cone into his mouth, folded in his wings, and cannonballed into the pool. Several reporters got drenched.

"There's your answer," Angel said.

"How old are you? Are you all related?" A woman held a microphone toward Nudge.

"We're...fifteen, twelve, nine, and seven," Nudge said, still getting used to their new ages. "Gazzy and Angel are the only real brother and sister."

"You weren't all from the same egg, so to speak?" asked another reporter, causing laughter.

Nudge looked at him. "Do we *look* like we're all from the same egg?" She pointed to Iggy, who was very pale skinned. She herself was at least partly African American. Gazzy and Angel both had cornsilk-yellow hair, ivory skin, and blue eyes.

"Where's Maximum? And the tall dark boy? We've seen them in pictures," someone said.

"They're busy right now and couldn't be here," said Angel smoothly.

"Who's the new member?" a woman asked Dylan.

"I'm a friend of the family," Dylan responded casually. "Birds of a feather, you know."

Everyone laughed, and flashes popped as he smiled. Then the cameras clicked some more. They couldn't get enough of him.

"Do you have any other special talents?" a reporter yelled.

Angel looked right at him. "No."

"But Angel—that's not true," Dylan said.

Angel glared at him. She should have gone over some flock rules with him. She should have thought of this. Now she had to fix it.

60

"DYLAN," BEGAN ANGEL, sounding firm.

"Dylan?" Jeb asked, walking over to him with an urgent look.

"...'Cause I can sing," finished Dylan, standing up.

"Oh, lordy, spare me the karaoke!" Total muttered, trotting over to sit in the shade beneath a patio table.

"You were in the rain, I saw you there," Dylan sang. Angel recognized the words of a song that had been playing incessantly on the radio. "I want to kiss the rain, and your sorrow, from your hair...."

"Well, butter my butt and call me a biscuit," Total murmured. "That kid can actually carry a tune."

Angel sat back on her lounge chair and grinned. The

reporters were eating this up, taking pictures, yelling questions. She was going to ask for more money.

Gazzy jumped up and stood behind Dylan, adding a beat box layer to the song. Iggy began drumming on a table with his hands. Nudge began singing backup and harmony, the way Angel had heard her do a million times, along with the radio.

"Give me your pain, I can take it." Dylan jumped up on a bench by the pool and spread his wings. "Give me your heart, I won't break it."

"I won't breeeaak it," Nudge echoed, her voice sounding great with Dylan's.

Total edged out from under the table and threw back his head to join in, but Angel tapped him with her foot. He glared at her. "Don't overshadow the others," Angel whispered. "Let them have this." Total's glare faded and he nodded magnanimously.

Problem averted, and they sounded dang good, Angel thought. What if...they became a family band? Like in *The Sound of Music*? Angel pictured them becoming rich and famous—famous for something other than being freaks. Maybe her plan to bring the flock into "a new era of peace and prosperity," as her Voice had called it, was really going to work.

But if it was such a great idea, why was she feeling so *sick*?

She looked at the others. Their song was winding

down, and they were smiling and bowing to the cheering crowd . . . but Nudge looked pale.

"Jeb? Could you get rid of the reporters? We need to rest before the concert tonight." Being a leader was coming naturally, she had to admit. She knew how to delegate — unlike Max, who only knew how to give orders.

"Okay, that's enough for now," Jeb said, starting to wave the reporters away. He motioned to the security team to clear the area, and they went into action.

"I feel like crap," complained Gazzy. "And it's not my digestive system this time."

"Tell me about it. I have the spins," said Nudge, sinking onto her chair and closing her eyes.

"I feel like I ate some rotten escargot. So much for the joys of room service," Total grumbled, lying down with his head next to Akila's paws. His lady friend seemed fine.

"Try not to yak in the pool," Angel advised, even though she was having a hard time not doing it herself. "We need to make a good impression."

Jeb felt their foreheads, the way he had a long time ago. "No fever. But you all feel bad? What did you have for lunch? Did you all eat the same thing?"

"Uh-oh," said Gazzy, but Angel was so nauseated she didn't have time to leap to a safe distance, or grab a gas mask.

Bbbbbrrrrrrrrttthhhhhhhttttttt.

"Mother of God, no!" Total cried, doing a fast belly-crawl

to the pool and throwing himself in. "You said it wasn't your digestive system!"

"What was that?" Dylan asked. He winced and threw an arm over his nose and mouth. "Another nerve gas bomb?"

"Sorry," Gazzy said miserably, but he couldn't help a tiny grin.

Nudge was clawing at a stack of towels to cover her face.

"Nice one, Gaz," said Iggy. "You know, I just thought of something: It's only us who're sick. Not the normal ones, like Jeb and Akila—only the recombined ones."

"Wait—that was Gazzy? Is that why you call him...Oh, crap," said Dylan weakly.

Angel stood up, but her balance was a little off. "I think we should all...," she began, and then the world faded and went topsy-turvy, before everything went black.

61

THE WAITRESS at the all-day breakfast buffet brought me four more pancakes, looking at me doubtfully.

"Yay, thanks," I said, making room on my plate. "You want that last sausage?" I said to Fang.

He pushed it over to me. "Okay, what's wrong?"

I quit chewing. "What?"

"You hardly got any sleep last night, your flying has been erratic and clumsy all day, and you're slowing down after only twelve pancakes. What's on your mind?"

"You really do know me," I said, and swallowed. Although—"Wait a minute. My flying was clumsy? I don't think so."

Fang grinned at me, with predictable heart-fluttery results.

"Okay," I said. I poured myself a lake of maple syrup and started pushing triangular rafts of pancake into it. "I've been thinking. Angel said that you were gonna die. Then Dylan shows up, Mr. Perfect. Jeb comes back into our lives. Angel boots me out of the flock. Dr. God is now everywhere, and there's someone shooting at us. What if Angel and Dr. G-H are working together? Or he's controlling her somehow?"

Fang stared at me blankly and then looked out the window.

"What if it's all part of some larger plan?" I continued, keeping my voice down. "Like, someone's trying to split up the flock. Or Jeb is trying to take over again, and can't with me there. Or you," I amended. As a rock-solid hypothesis—ha-ha—it wasn't much.

Fang pushed food around on his plate. "Mr. Perfect?" was his only comment.

"What? Oh." My stomach knotted. "No—I mean, it's just like he's a Ken doll or something. Mutant Ken, with wings. Like he was designed to be..."

"Perfect?" Fang's gaze was level.

"*Someone's* idea of perfect," I said. "Not *mine*, obviously."

"Yeah," said Fang. Awkward silence. "Or...it could all just be a bunch of weird stuff happening for no reason. Here's the non-conspiracy-theory version: Dr. God is just an egomaniac. Angel is just another one in the making. Jeb and Dylan are just a couple of losers looking for a family.

And maybe you were just a pain-in-the-butt leader and the kids kicked you out for good reason."

My eyebrows rose, and Fang gave me a lopsided grin before I could shoot him down.

"Or maybe not," he admitted. "Maybe we should call, check in?"

"I still feel responsible for them." I sighed. "Even though they're, you know, all backstabbing little ingrates."

Fang nodded, and his too-long black hair swished like silk.

"I'll call Nudge," I decided. "She seemed kind of the least turncoaty."

Holding my breath, I dialed Nudge's number. If she hung up on me or told me not to call anymore, it would be very bad. I hesitated, thinking this through.

"Just hit send," said Fang.

So I did. It rang for a long time. What were they do—

"Hello?" Nudge sounded so normal I wanted to cry.

"Hey, Nudge. It's me." I cleared my throat and braced myself. There was a lot of noise on her end, people talking, a TV blaring. I heard Gazzy laughing in the background. "'Ssup?"

"Max!" Nudge sounded thrilled to hear from me. "Max, hi! Where are you?"

That was weird. She knew I wouldn't say anything over the phone. "Where are *you*?" I asked as a test.

"LA!" she said. "We're going to a party with celebrities!"

"Huh. Um, are you okay?"

"We all had, like, stomach flu earlier. But now we're fine. I miss you! Oops, limo's here! Gotta go. Love you! Call ya later!" She hung up.

I looked at Fang. "They're fine. Going to a party with celebrities in LA. Limo was there to pick them up."

Fang looked at me. "Trap?"

I nodded. "Oh, yeah. Trap."

62

THE LIMO PULLED to a stop outside Furioso, the hottest, most exclusive restaurant in Los Angeles. Needless to say, it wasn't dog friendly, so the canines had stayed back at the hotel. There was a crowd of people on the sidewalk.

The flock gazed out the darkened windows of the limo. This was pretty much the farthest situation from anything that Max would have agreed to. They were surrounded, trapped in a car driven by a stranger, with tons of people taking pictures.

"Are you sure this is a good idea?" Jeb asked.

That was enough to decide it for Angel. "Yep. It's show-time, folks," she said, popping her door open. The flock heard murmurs ripple through the crowd. Then people were jostling, trying to get closer, trying to see them as they spilled out of the limo.

"It's the bird kids!" Flashes went off like a hundred tiny fireworks.

Nudge gave a big smile, posing for the cameras. "Hello," she said, changing her angles. Dylan looked down at first but couldn't help giving shy smiles to the adoring onlookers. Gazzy bounced up and down and waved.

"Get me out of here," said Iggy, whose superior sensory skills normally made him comfortable weaving his way through any scene of chaos. "This is giving me the willies."

Angel looked at him, surprised. "Everything is fine," she said firmly. "Let's go inside." The crowd parted around her as if she had waved a magic wand. With her enhanced raptor vision, Angel could see everything in the smoky darkness as they weaved through the restaurant.

Their contact, a talk show host named Madeline Hammond, ran forward, her hands out.

"Kids!" she said, beaming a thousand-watt smile. "Thanks so much for coming! Hey, give us a little room, will ya?" she called to the crowd, and people edged back. "Welcome to the pre-party! Isn't this great? The Harrells are going to play later, and Beth Duncraft and Fala Cochran are here." Her gaze fell on Dylan just then, and she looked up into his turquoise eyes. "Oh, my goodness," she said slowly. "Who are you?"

"I'm Dylan," he said. "The new bird kid on the block."

Madeline looked stunned, then recovered herself, turning to speak to the crowd. "They sure can make 'em, right, folks? Is this guy gorgeous or what?" The crowd roared its approval. Madeline smiled. "All of you are just fantastic!"

Nudge squealed with delight. She turned and posed again, waving.

"Let me introduce you to some people," said Madeline Hammond, and for the next twenty minutes, Angel was absorbed in a blur of smiles and air kisses and shaking hands. But with every passing moment, noises seemed to grow louder, colors seemed to get brighter, and her skin felt more and more itchy and tight.

She glanced at Nudge, who was beaming up into the face of a boy currently starring in a popular sitcom. He looked about sixteen, and Angel grinned, wondering if he knew that, despite her height, Nudge was only elev—twelve.

"And how did you learn to fly?" a reporter asked Dylan.

"I got pushed off a roof," he said truthfully. The crowd laughed, eating him up.

In the darkness, Angel saw Gazzy and Iggy sitting at the restaurant's bar, taking turns flicking almonds into glasses as if it were an advanced game of tiddlywinks. Several Hollywood writer-producer types seemed to be regressing to childhood as they joined the competition, guffawing with the boys and making a scene.

Dylan was surrounded by slinky, admiring girls, some of whom Angel recognized from TV. He was smiling, talking, turning on his own star quality, but Angel thought his expression looked strained, and his skin pale and clammy.

Dylan + pale skin = ? *Does not compute.*

And that's when it occurred to her. Dylan always looked perfect. Even when he'd just been shredded by Erasers.

There was something very wrong with him. With all of them.

That was when Angel looked down at her hands, seeing them clearly in the dim light. And she screamed.

63

"MA'AM, YOU SHOULD SEE THIS." The tech nervously pointed at the surveillance screen.

The head of information stared at the face of Subject 6. It was covered with huge oozing pustules, like boils. The subject was crying, even as she tried to keep from scratching her skin raw. There was much activity in the area as the other subjects started to gather around number 6.

"Have you seen Twenty-two yet?" the head asked.

"Yes," the tech replied grimly, just as the subject in question came into view. The tech enhanced the night-vision capabilities of the camera. Subject 22 was indeed also covered with the plaguelike skin lesions.

"Another malfunction. Unbelievable," the head of information whispered. "This couldn't have been from the reactant. It was tested a hundred times. We know the effect it has. It couldn't have done this. In fact—I believe it was tested on Twenty-two himself when he was six months old. Check the records on that before I inform the doctor."

The tech nodded.

"ASAP," the head pressed. "The doctor is going to be very, very upset when he—" She broke off and squinted at the screen. There seemed to be some kind of commotion. People pressing together, people yelling.

"What's going on now?"

The tech turned up the volume and tried refocusing the camera. "It may be that one of the subjects just collapsed? I'm not sure. Let me come in closer...."

"We have to get field reports!" the head yelled, pulling out her phone to mobilize the street team. "This could be turning into an emergency scenario. We are not going to lose any of the subjects on my watch."

64

I'M NOT CLAIRVOYANT or anything. I can't read minds or pick up on stray thoughts the way Angel can. But I know where Los Angeles is, and I can read a huge blinking sign that says "Bird kids here tonight! Come meet the flock! Get your tickets at TicketsPlus!"

I pointed, and Fang nodded. "It's a thin clue, but I say we follow it," I said. We angled downward, avoiding cell towers and trying not to breathe in the smog, which you could have cut with a knife and spread on toast. Not that you'd want to.

The sign was perched atop a four-story building that looked as if it had once been a movie theater. On the ground floor was a restaurant called Furioso. Signs on the sidewalk proclaimed the opportunity to talk to "Nature's Marvels, Today Only."

"*Nature* had nothing to do with it," I muttered.

"Good thing the kids are keeping a low profile," Fang commented.

As we got closer to Furioso, people started streaming out the front doors, yelling and screaming. Burly bouncers were trying to control them, but no one can withstand the kick of a Jimmy Choo stiletto in the shin.

We waited a moment, but the flock wasn't among the escapees. Which meant they were inside. I didn't even have to think, just dived between designer-clad bodies.

"No one goes in!" a bouncer said, looming large in front of me. "Everyone's clearing out!"

"We've got VIP passes," I told him. Fang and I spread our wings. "Up and away!" We catapulted into the air and flew right over him as he looked up at us in a daze.

After that, LA's young and restless got out of our way.

Inside, it was dark enough to hide most face-lifts, but it took only a moment to locate the flock—they were standing by the one light source in the place. I also spotted Jeb's sandy hair. At the same time, I took in the fact that three people dressed in black were converging on the flock, and they didn't look like hospitality associates.

I nodded at Fang, and he broke away, circling behind them as I pulled back into the shadows. Nudge sniffled and caught sight of me. I was shocked to see that her eyes were almost swollen shut. I glimpsed the others' faces and noticed weird spots and swelling. WTH?

I put a finger to my lips, then circled it in the air. Nudge nodded almost imperceptibly, reaching behind her to tap Iggy's hand twice. He tapped Gazzy's hand twice, and Gazzy stopped blinking back tears and went quietly on alert.

So pretty much everyone was already primed by the time the biggest guy reached Jeb, pulled a gun out of his coat, and jabbed it into Jeb's side.

"Nobody move!" the guy barked. "You're all going to come with us! Somebody wants to see you."

"I don't think anyone wants to see us looking like *this*," said Dylan.

The woman closest to him whirled, also pulling out a gun. In less time than it takes to tell, Dylan chopped the gun out of her hand, then grabbed her, locking her arms behind her back. So smoothly, so professionally, it was almost as though he had known she was coming.

Immediately, I swept my foot under the third one's shoes, knocking him off balance, then clapped my hands hard over his ears. He shrieked in pain as his eardrums popped, and he fell. I planted my foot firmly on his neck, ready to stomp if he moved a muscle.

Meanwhile...

Almost as if in slow motion...

The gun skidded across the floor. And guess which of

us had her bird kid claws all over that grisly weapon in the blink of an eye?

You got it. The scary seven-year-old with a leadership complex.

Having been subjected to the threat of guns way too many times in our short lives, the flock were not fans of them. Didn't touch them, didn't believe in them, didn't want anything to do with them. And, fortunately, didn't have a shred of experience using them.

So looking at Angel holding a gun? It wasn't just terrifying. It was tragic. I felt crushed by the horror of what our lives had come to.

My sweet little Angel, looking like a murderer in a pink party dress.

I might say this a lot, but: This was like my worst nightmare. For real this time.

But then it got worse.

Because when Angel lifted the gun, she pointed it at me.

65

"NOBODY MOVES UNTIL I TELL them to," Angel said calmly, as if she'd been doing this—or at least watching R-rated Mafia movies after I'd gone to sleep—her whole life.

I must admit, as a tactic the shock factor was super effective. Everyone was frozen with disbelief. For a moment, it was as if we were all on the same team, trying to talk a psycho down from the ledge. Every single one of us wanted that gun out of that child's hands.

The scary thing was, she didn't look like a child anymore. She looked very, very focused. And I was very, very focused on the barrel of the gun.

"Put it down," the guy holding Jeb told her. "You don't know what you're doing."

"Yes, she does," said Dylan seriously.

"Well, then, what does she *think* she's doing?" the woman he had captive asked through clenched teeth.

"Okay, so what happens next is that everyone shuts up and listens to what I have to say," Angel demanded.

Tell me to shut up, and I speak. "I'm listening, Angel. I simply cannot *wait* to hear this one."

She gave me a look. *Listen to me, Max.*

"One by one, and only when I say," Angel began, "the grown-ups will turn around and walk away without hurting us. And if you don't do it, I'll pull the trigger. And then what happens?"

"You'll kill Max," Fang said hoarsely.

"Right." Her grip, her arm, didn't waver. "And you grown-ups know as well as I do that Max is the prize. The only prize that really matters to your boss. You know exactly who I'm talking about. He would be very, very mad if she died and it was your fault, wouldn't he? That would be very, very bad for you. Wouldn't it?"

"You wouldn't kill a member of your own flock. You'd never do it!" the guy whose neck was under my foot cried from the floor.

"Is that what you think?" Angel smiled. "Max, what do you think?"

I only needed to consider for a millisecond. "No question about it," I said, staring her down. "She would do it."

"Give us one good reason why we should believe that!" squawked Dylan's captive.

"In case you guys didn't catch last week's episode, I'm out of the flock," I informed them, letting my voice shake as much as possible. "Angel has no allegiance to me. She's wanted me gone for a long time. And in case you didn't catch all of the episodes from the past year, Angel is...unbalanced."

"Untrustworthy," Fang seconded.

"Unpredictable," Jeb added.

"Dangerous," Dylan chimed in. The other kids were, thankfully, too scared to speak up.

"Right," Angel said slowly. "That's just the word I would use. But I think everyone understands that now. So, Dylan, you can let your lady there go. She's under control. Nice and easy, ma'am. Just turn around and walk away."

As Dylan slowly loosened his grip, the woman's eyes glazed over, and zombie-like, she headed out of the restaurant. Angel's gaze was back on me now, strong and steady.

"Max, I think the gentleman under your foot is ready now. Bye-bye. Leave. Don't ever come looking for us again," she told him firmly.

Even after seeing Angel in action all these years, I was still awed by her powers as I lifted my foot and watched the man peel himself from the floor and stumble out.

"And finally, you, sir, with the gun. You're going to leave now without hurting any of us bird kids. Go home and forget everything that just happened. Okay?"

"Okay," he said, with a bizarre expression on his face.

Then he pulled the trigger.

There was a pop, and Jeb collapsed. The rest of us gasped in horror.

"I didn't hurt any of you bird kids," he said emotionlessly. "Just like you said."

Looking dazed, he dropped his gun to the floor and ran out.

66

JEB ALWAYS SAID HE'D TAKE a bullet for us. Now that he had, it significantly changed my sense of superiority over him. If he died, I would have some major soul-searching to do. Advice: Don't wait until someone you have issues with—especially someone you're related to—gets *shot* before you work it out.

Fortunately, the bullet seemed to have missed the important parts, but he'd lost a lot of blood, so there was no way we could avoid the dreaded hospital. I'd rather be in a zoo. Instead I was in a waiting room, taking out my frustrations on a vending machine that wasn't working. I really needed some chocolate.

"Max!" I heard someone call. I felt my stomach unknot slightly.

"Mom!" I hurried to her, and we hugged. I'm not a huggy person, but her hugs were pretty much the best hugs on earth.

"Jeb's out of surgery," she said. "It looks like he'll be fine."

Fang and I led my mom to a room where the rest of the flock was under observation. The "agents" that Angel had hired had set up their private security guys outside the door—they didn't want word of this leaking out. These kids were no longer marketable.

"Dr. Martinez!" Nudge said, managing a weak smile. Mom was good about not grimacing. Nudge's skin looked like chocolate pudding bubbling in a pot on the stove. The rest looked like they had been dipped in a cauldron of lye. Doctors had swabbed the flock's sores, taken blood, taken their temperatures—but hadn't found squat.

"Oh, my gosh, Nudge," my mom said gently. She smoothed some of Nudge's corkscrew curls off her forehead, then went around and said hi to everyone else.

"I'm Dylan," Dylan said when she paused by his bed, looking confused.

"He's the latest, um, acquisition," I explained weakly. Even with his messed-up skin, he still looked like he'd been designed by Gods R Us. Except right now it was Trolls R Us. But, like, a troll who would totally be a pinup in all the troll teen magazines.

"Hi, Dylan," my mom said. "I'm Valencia Martinez, Max's mom."

Dylan's puffy eyes widened. "You have a *mother*?" he asked me. "Wow. I had no idea. Do you have a father too, then?"

Bad, bad question. My mom quickly changed the subject. "You know, I read about a case where someone poisoned a spy with a radioactive element," she said. "The pictures I saw kind of looked like this."

"Oh, holy crap," I said, putting my hand to my mouth.

"It's not radiation poisoning," said a voice.

"Jeb!" My mom went over and closed the door behind him.

"How do you know?" I demanded of Jeb. "Did you have something to do with this?"

"No," said Jeb. He was wearing a hospital gown, open in the back, and I hoped he was enjoying the breeze. An IV dripped into his arm, and he had wheeled its little stand in with him. He looked pale and weak—after all, he *had* taken a bullet for us. Maybe I should be a *tad* less accusatory.

"No," he repeated. "And I hope I'm wrong, but I think it's an…accelerator of some kind. A genetic accelerator."

"What the heck is that?" Gazzy asked.

Jeb paused. "Well…it's something that would react with your genes. Basically introducing new mutations and speeding up mutations you already have. I think all of us got dosed, except maybe Max and Fang, because they were gone. But it's having an effect only on you, whose DNA has already been modified."

There was an appalled silence. I'd been gone for, like, two days, and in that time, everything had completely careened out of control.

"But what if it helps us become even *better*?" Angel said, ever the creepy optimist. Her normally beautiful face looked like a personal-size pizza with eyes. "We could be like superheroes!"

"Yeah, so far that's working out well for you," I said, gesturing to everyone's ruined skin. "Do you have any idea who would—" I stopped as the obvious answer came to me. "Dr. Seersucker."

Angel sat up. "Dr. Gunther-Hagen is really brilliant, Max."

"You want to be accelerated? Fine. But you have no idea what's going to happen to you next. We already know that your good doctor's self-healing genetics can have some pretty scary side effects."

Angel frowned, and Dylan looked concerned. I'd forgotten he had been gifted with Dr. Gunther-Hagen's magic spit.

My mom turned to Jeb, who was leaning against a wall, looking gray. "Is there any way to know what will happen to them? How toxic is it? Is it deadly? Is there any way to get it out of their systems?"

"Um, not really, I'm not sure, I don't think so, and I doubt it," said Jeb, trying to answer all her questions. "My guess is that this initial bad reaction might be the shock of having it introduced to their systems. I'm hoping that once it's absorbed, these side effects will go away."

"This was someone conducting an experiment," Fang said slowly. Frowning, he turned to Jeb. "Someone who'd want to be there to see the results."

Jeb held up a hand. "Don't even go there, Fang. The accelerant would have had to be in a shared source—say, in the air or water at the house. I would have been affected too."

"But it wouldn't affect you because you're normal," Fang objected. "You said so yourself."

"That's just a theory," Jeb said. "This was not my doing."

My mom interjected. "Let's focus on the important thing here. Is there a way to undo this?"

Jeb shook his head. "If I'm right, it would have been designed to start binding to their DNA immediately, inserting its enzymes and amino acids directly into their chromosomes."

I sank down onto a hard plastic chair. "Oh, my God."

"This could give us cancer!" Nudge said, blinking back tears.

"Or turn us into, like, pterodactyls or something," said Gazzy. "It wouldn't take much." He looked stoic.

Jeb sighed. "We should contact Gunther-Hagen to see if he admits to any of this—or even if he won't admit it, maybe he'll give us clues as to what it is."

The idea of contacting the doc for *help* was totally crazy

to me. Excuse me, but hadn't Jeb just been *shot* by one of the man's employees?

"I would vote to get out of here, get to a safe house, and see what happens over the next twenty-four hours," I suggested.

"I'll call a contact at the CSM," said my mom, reaching for her phone. "He'll be able to help us find a place."

But I had only one real desire right then: to go back to Colorado and drink the water. If my flock was going through this, I needed to go through it too.

BOOK FOUR

THE TOTALLY, COMPLETELY UNTHINKABLE

67

TOTAL WAS GLAD TO SEE us all again. His own horrible skin lesions were somewhat disguised by his black fur, but he was definitely suffering the same effects.

"I feel like crap!" he said, once we were settled at the new safe house. "At first I thought I'd gotten some bad shrimp dip, but this is way beyond that."

"How's Akila?" I asked. "She seem okay?"

"Yes, thank God." His small black eyes glittered. "Which reminds me. I've got some big news—"

"Max? Come look at this sunset," said Dylan. I'd been avoiding him ever since we got here, even though I'd felt his eyes on me whenever we were in the same room. Nudge had told me he was a great singer and could totally be a star, on top of being a great fighter who got along swimmingly with the rest of the flock.

Without meaning to, I glanced across the room at Fang, who'd been talking to Gazzy and Iggy. His gaze was lasered in on me.

"Oh, I'm sure it's great," I said to Dylan lamely. The picture window showed the low mountains off in the distance, and we could see a bit of the ocean if we leaned way to the left on the balcony.

"You don't know what you're missing," said Dylan, a wistful smile on his slightly less troll-like face. "But I'd understand if you want to keep your distance from"—he pointed at himself—"this mess."

"Can't you, like, put some magic spit on it and make it all better?" I asked, only half joking.

"Tried it already." He chuckled. "I guess even the doc's magic doesn't work on bad teenage complexions. I'm doomed."

The irony of Dylan complaining about his usually perfect skin was not lost on me. I laughed, then smothered it, not willing to be sucked into his charm.

The rest of the flock was starting to seem better too, as Jeb had predicted. They had more energy, and their skin looked less awful. If Jeb was right, their systems were absorbing the reactant, binding it to their genes, and soon it would be normal, a part of them. Greeaaaat. I kept waiting for antlers to pop out of their heads or for them to start understanding Akila when she barked. I mean, what the heck was going to happen to them?

The next day the skin lesions were virtually gone. But we hardly even noticed because, lo and behold, something else was gone too.

Angel.

Do you want to join me in the next word? Okay, everyone all together now:

Again.

It wasn't like the other times, when we had to mobilize our forces and piece together clues and leap out into the air on a rescue mission.

This time, we only had to read the note.

Dear Flock and Max and Dr. Martinez and Jeb and Dylan,

You guys are wrong about Dr. Hans. He wants to help us, and for us to be the best we can be. You don't trust him because you don't trust anybody. But I want to be more powerful. I want to know what he's working on. I've gone to work with him. Please don't follow me. Things will only get messy if you do.

Love,

Angel

P.S. I just want to remind you that Fang's time is about up. Him being there puts the rest of the flock in danger. I'm sorry, Fang.

68

"CAN'T WE PUT a boot on her, like a little car?" Gazzy asked, rubbing his hair in frustration so that it stood straight up.

"Yeah, maybe we should start locking her in at night," I said wryly.

"Could she have been...kidnapped?" my mom asked.

We all quickly looked around. There was no sign of disturbance; everything was still locked. And the note was in Angel's handwriting.

"No, I think she decided to go," I said. "As much as I wish that weren't true."

"What does she mean about Fang's time being up?" Jeb asked.

"She said that in Africa," said Nudge. "She said Fang was gonna die."

"Die?" My mom's eyes widened.

"She was just trying to get attention," said Fang. "It doesn't mean anything."

I suddenly had a thought, one of those awful thoughts that you hate right away and yet you can't ever unthink it. I felt my heart start to pound as I stood up.

"Fang? Let me see the back of your neck."

Those of us who graduated from (or, I should say, *escaped* from) the School have expiration dates, like milk. We first noticed them on some Erasers, after they had...expired. Dates, like little tattoos, showed up on the backs of their necks. They seem to become visible about a week, maybe less, before the built-in expiration gene kicks in. Do we have long, full lives ahead of us, or are we living on borrowed time? No clue. It makes retirement planning, like, impossible.

Fang stood up. In the past year he'd gotten taller than I was, so I had to stand on tiptoe a bit to see his neck. I didn't want to look—didn't want to know. I couldn't even let myself think of what it would mean if I saw a date there.

But I'm not a coward. So I brushed his black silky hair off the smooth skin of his neck—the same neck I had kissed not long ago. I could smell his clean Fang smell, the one he inexplicably had even when he was noticeably filthy and covered in gore.

And I looked.

And saw...just smooth, plain, tan Fang skin. I let out a breath I didn't know I'd been holding.

"No date," I quickly told the others, and they visibly relaxed.

"Do I have a date?" Dylan's quiet voice almost made me jump—I'd forgotten that he was there.

"I don't know," I said. "You were made by different people, I think."

Uncertainty played across his once-again-gorgeous face.

I took pity on him. "I could...look. I guess."

He came to stand close to me, and turned his back. His streaky blond hair wasn't as long as Fang's, but I still had to push it out of the way. And tug down a tiny bit on the neck of his maroon T-shirt. I hadn't been this close to Dylan before, and I realized that he smelled good in a completely different way. Clean. Spicy.

Then I realized what I was thinking, and my cheeks burned. I took a fast look at his neck and snatched my hands away. "No date. Not that that means anything."

"At least you don't have one," said my mom. "We know what having one means; we don't know what not having one means."

Still, Angel's note had reignited the fears I'd tried to bury. What if all of the attacks in recent days had been meant for Fang? The Eraser attack, the Cirque shooter, the Furioso incident—what if all of these had been designed to get Fang? I remembered how Dylan had chopped the woman's gun out of her hand at the restaurant.

He just might have saved Fang's life.

69

"WHERE DOES DR. GOD hang out?" I asked. "Where exactly has Angel gone? How did she know where to find him?"

Nudge headed to our computer. "On it."

"I'll go with you," Fang told me, already starting to load his pockets with knives, throwing stars, Snickers bars.

"No," I said, trying to sound calm. "I'll go by myself."

He straightened up, and let me tell you, it was all I could do not to crumble and beg him to come with me. Any fight was possible with Fang as my backup. Any trip was more fun. But what if this was all designed to get *him*? I just didn't know. I couldn't take that chance. The thought of anything happening to Fang... it was much worse than thinking of anything happening to me.

Fang, typically, didn't start pelting me with questions. Instead he looked at me, cocked his head slightly, and thought things through.

"You think you'll have more chance of success without me?" he asked mildly.

"No," I answered honestly. "Of course not. But I'm willing to risk me. I'm not willing to risk you."

He opened his mouth to start arguing, but I held up my hand. "Fang, we don't know what this whole 'Fang's time is up' thing is about. But if it turns out that Angel's doing *this* as part of *that,* then I don't want to make it easy for them. You know?"

I turned to Jeb. After the shooting incident, I felt I had to trust him more. "Are you going to be staying here for a while?" I asked him.

He nodded.

"You can't go by yourself, Max," said Dylan.

I blinked. I mean, I don't take direction from people I *love,* so direction from people I've practically just met? Not likely.

"Um, I found an address in Malibu, weirdly enough," said Nudge.

"Malibu?" I frowned. "That's practically next door."

"Max, what if something happens to you?" Dylan asked.

I ignored him and turned back to Jeb. "If Fang is in any way harmed while I'm gone—if he gets a *hangnail*—you won't see another morning. Are we clear on that?"

Fang crossed his arms over his chest. "This is ridiculous. I've never needed a babysitter."

"Not a babysitter—just backup," I told him. "Iggy, Nudge, and Gazzy are also on duty here. But I don't think I'll be gone long."

I moved to leave, and Dylan actually grabbed my shoulders. I was so surprised that I forgot to karate-chop his elbows and break his arms.

"I don't want anything to happen to you," he said urgently.

"What you want does not matter here," I said slowly and carefully. I hoped Dylan was sensitive enough to read between the lines, to the subtext of: *Let go of me or I'll kill you.*

He let go of me. Fang was looking at him with narrowed eyes. I didn't have time for this.

"Okay, later," I said, and strode off to save the day, once again. I hoped.

70

DR. HANS GUNTHER-HAGEN left his computer console and headed out to the terrace overlooking the ocean.

"Max is on the way," he said. "I thought it would take longer for her to find this house."

"Nah," said Angel, dunking a strawberry into her non-alcoholic strawberry daiquiri. "They're totally on top of the research, especially with that government computer."

"Government computer?"

"Yeah. From the CIA or the NSA or something," Angel said. She lay back on her patio lounger and adjusted her sunglasses. Her pure white wings were spread out to the sides, about nine feet across. The sunlight warmed the feathers, soaking in to heat the porous, light bones. It felt fantastic.

"She should be here quite soon," said Dr. Hans. He shaded his eyes and searched the sky, as if even now he'd be able to see her tiny silhouette against the blue.

"Yeah," said Angel, setting down her drink and closing her eyes. "I told you."

She listened to the doctor walk away, hearing every nuance of his steps. She smiled to herself but made sure to keep it off her face. This was why Max liked being the leader, she thought. It was amazing to figure out a plan and then have it work, just watch it all start to fall into place. It was like playing chess, but with real people. And the endgame was about to start.

71

MALIBU WAS BUILT on cliffs next to the Pacific Ocean. There was a narrow strip of dark tan sand, then a thin row of houses, then the Pacific Coast Highway, then cliffs dotted with more houses. I have one word, people: *earthquake.* I mean, hello, San Andreas Fault? Those houses would be toast crumbs if the big one hit.

Dr. Gunther-Hagen's house was overlooking the beach— I recognized it from the satellite photos Nudge had found. I held my breath and dropped down onto his terrace, hoping everyone around had their eyes glued to the hypnotic waves and the even more hypnotic all-girl beach volleyball competition taking place down on the sand.

The first thing I saw—well, after a quick sweep to

check out security teams, cameras, razor wire, etc.—was Angel, lounging on a...lounger.

"Hi, Max," she said, pushing her shades up onto her curls.

"I hope you're wearing sunscreen," I said. "You're gonna have hella wrinkles by the time you're ten."

"Want some daiquiri?" she offered, pointing at a blender.

"Is it traitor flavored?" I asked.

Angel sighed and sat up as the sliding glass doors opened. Dr. Hans Gunther-Hagen came out, dressed in a crisp white linen suit. He smiled and held out his hands to me.

"Maximum!" he said. "I'm so glad you've come to join us."

"Whoa, let's get one thing straight, Hansie," I said, keeping a healthy distance from him. "I came here for answers. I'm not joining nobody."

"That's a double negative, Max," Angel noted. If I was the one who had taught her grammar, I now regretted it.

"Max, please, sit down," said Dr. G-H. He gestured to a patio chair. I crossed my arms over my chest and looked at him.

"What are you using Angel for?" I asked. "And what's Fang got to do with it?"

"Max," said Angel, "there isn't much time left for the world as we know it. If we want to survive, we have to join Dr. Hans and work with him."

"I'm going to take my chances surviving without him," I told her. "Didn't you read your Evil-Scientist Manual?

I'm pretty sure this whole setup was mentioned on page seventy-eight."

"You can't joke about this, Max," Angel said earnestly, and I refrained from pointing out that I just had. "You have your Voice, and I have mine. We have to listen to them."

"I don't know about *your* so-called Voice, Angel, but if it's anything like mine, I can tell you this," I said. "We can *learn* from them, if they don't seem nuts, but we're still supposed to be making our own decisions. Trust me on this."

"Max, things are going to get bad very soon," said Dr. Hans. "We'll have to function in a world that we can barely imagine — a frightening and primitive one. But there's still time to save yourself. You and the rest of the flock. It's not too late."

"Yeah, and all I have to do is divorce myself from any ethical standards whatsoever and jump onto the Untrustworthy Control Freak bandwagon," I said. "No, thanks."

"All you *have* to do is let go of Fang," said Dr. G-H. "Do that, and everyone else survives."

I stared at him. "No can do, Hans. Nonnegotiable."

"Are you saying you'd let Fang and the others *die* just because you're being stubborn? Just because you won't accept Dylan instead? Is he not a worthy suitor for our Maximum Ride? Tell me, Max: what's wrong with him?"

Well. He had me there. "He's too...clean?" I offered weakly.

Dr. Gunnie-Hunnie looked like a disappointed parent. "We worked very hard to make him just right for you,

Max. You haven't even let him get close enough to find out just how very…wonderful he could be for you."

What was that supposed to mean?

I was quiet. Quiet some more. And all confused-like. "Well, it's been swell. Gotta go."

"Max, please," said Angel. "Save yourself. Save the others. Please."

"You have two seconds to get up and come with me," I said to her. "But I'm leaving. If the world is about to come to an end, I want to spend my last days with my family."

"I'm staying here," Angel said sadly.

This was it? I was really losing her? Forever?

It was a strangely mucked-up feeling. It seemed like yesterday that I was cuddling her when she was upset during thunderstorms. It was also just days ago when she was holding a gun on me. I didn't know who she was anymore. But I hoped that my old Angel was still inside there somewhere, and that she would break free of whatever forces had taken her over.

I swallowed and nodded.

"Max, I could keep you here by force," said Dr. God, steel in his voice. He nodded, and suddenly four armed guards stepped out of nowhere and pointed guns at me. Angel bit her lip. Quelle surprise.

I made a face at him. "Yeah, but what's the fun of that? Later. Enjoy the apocalypse." Then I ran across the terrace, jumped over the edge, and threw myself off the cliff. No bullets zinged past me. My flock was waiting.

72

"ARE YOU REALLY IN DANGER?" Dylan's voice broke into Fang's thoughts.

Fang looked at the newest bird kid. Dylan was an inch or two taller than he was, and somewhat heavier built, though he still had the long, lean look of a human-avian hybrid— you couldn't make bricks fly. "I don't know. Maybe."

"How can you stay here?" Dylan asked.

Fang stood and picked up his drink before he answered. "What do you mean?"

"If you're in danger, then someone's coming after you, right?" said Dylan. "And if you're standing right next to, say, Gazzy, then Gazzy's in danger too, right?"

"What are you getting at?"

"You're putting everyone else in danger," Dylan said gravely. "You're putting *Max* in danger. Doesn't it upset you?"

"I'm not going to discuss my feelings with you," Fang said. "I've got news for you, pal. Max has been in danger pretty much every day of her life, with a few notable exceptions. She knows how to deal with danger. We all do."

"Max isn't indestructible," Dylan persisted. "None of us are. If we can avoid danger, we should. We don't need to sit and wait for it to come."

Fang stared at him in a silence that felt less comfortable, less natural than usual.

"If I were you," said Dylan, "I'd be doing everything I could to keep Max safe." Some emotion crossed his face; Fang wasn't sure what it was. "But it's bigger than that," Dylan continued. "Max is the key to this whole flock surviving. According to Jeb, Max is the key to the whole *world* surviving. Sure, Angel was the leader for a couple days, and she's a strong kid. But she's no Max. The rest of the flock needs Max—more than *you* need her."

"I know that!" Fang was irritated now.

"Any one of us is dispensable," Dylan said. "If I disappear, I'm not even a blip on the screen. I know that. If you disappear, Max would be bummed, the flock would have lost a great fighter, but the flock would still be here. But without Max, how long do you think the flock would hold together? Even with you leading it? Would Dr. Martinez still be looking out for you? Would the CSM still be throwing houses your way? Would you have a single freaking clue about what to do?"

Dylan's voice had been steadily rising, and now he was focused on Fang, each word pelting him like a stone. The thing was, Fang thought, Dylan actually seemed sincere. He wasn't putting himself first.

On the other hand, if Fang listened to him and left the flock for its own good, and for Max's own good, it would be leaving the path wide open for Dylan to move in.

"You gotta do what you gotta do," said Dylan, calming down. "It's just—I can't stand the thought of something happening to Max. I can't stand it." His clear turquoise eyes met Fang's black ones. "I'm designed to feel that way."

Fang nodded. This guy had no artifice, no subterfuge. He didn't know enough to mask his thoughts or have secret plans or hidden motives. He was a sap, and he probably wouldn't last long.

"I'm gonna get something to eat," Fang said, and went inside, leaving Dylan by himself on the balcony. Fang's mind was blazing, but no one would be able to tell it.

73

DYLAN WAS CALMLY LEANING on the balcony rail of the safe house. His eyes were locked on me as soon as I came into view, as if he'd known exactly when I was returning.

"Max!" he shouted. "Glad to see you're okay." He pointed to a round table on the balcony. There, beckoning me, was a plate of chocolate chip cookies and a glass of milk. "Want some? Figured you'd be hungry after the flight."

How could he have known how much I loved chocolate chip cookies? I glowered at him. "Thanks but no thanks, Mr. Hospitality," I said, and walked right by the cookies. An incredible smell wafted from them—they were fresh from the oven.

In the living room, everything seemed normal—Gazzy and Iggy were playing a video game, Nudge was curled up with my mom reading a fashion magazine, Jeb was surfing the web on his computer, Total and Akila were asleep on the floor in the sun. And Fang was...

"Max! Did you find Angel?" my mom asked.

"Yes." I took a deep breath. "Angel's decided to stay with Dr. Guntha-Munka and help him with his research. She thinks that will give her the best chance."

"But she's okay?"

I nodded. "As okay as a crazy little monkey can be. I mean, she seems to be staying there by choice. She wouldn't come back with me."

Everyone was silent. I glanced around as they digested this info. "Where's Fang?"

"He's in our room," said Gazzy. "He's going to play the winner of Crash Test Four. Which will be me."

"I don't think so!" said Iggy, affronted. I guess Iggy had really been progressing in his "vision lessons."

I headed down the hall to talk to the one person who could make me feel better about the Angel situation.

I tapped on the door to their room, then opened it. The beds were empty. The door to the bathroom was open and the bathroom was empty. The window was open.

Then I saw the note. And my heart seemed to thud to a stop.

74

GIVE THIS NOTE TO MAX was hastily scrawled on the folded piece of paper. Fang's writing was always hasty, always scrawled. A beautiful mess. I opened it up.

Hey. Not sure what's going on — gonna go find out. Be careful and don't do anything stupid. Don't come after me — you're better on your own. See you. F.

I sat on the edge of the bed, holding the note.

Okay, so Fang had looked up *vague* in the dictionary, and this was what it had said to write. It could mean anything. So why was my heart thumping with fear?

Nudge came in. "I can't believe Angel's really gone," she

said. "She'll come back; I'm sure of it." Then she saw my face. "What's wrong? I mean, what else?"

I handed her the note.

She read it and frowned. "He left? He's gone too? When is he gonna be back?"

"Don't know," I managed to say.

Okay, if you've been reading about our adventures all along, you know me by now. You know that even in the face of the worst danger possible, I keep my head together and often manage a tart quip besides. It's part of being a leader.

But this note had really thrown me. I was so freaking sick of people leaving me and leaving little notes behind. And what did he mean, I was better on my own? On my own, like, *without him?* Was he *crazy?* Who was he to make that decision?

I felt frozen except for the burning hot tears starting to leak out.

"Max?" Nudge asked, sitting next to me. Her coffee-brown eyes were wide. She was used to seeing me leap into action, and my just sitting there looking like a stunned turtle was shocking enough, but she almost never saw me cry. No one did. I was tough. I was strong. I was a rock.

Meanwhile, I sort of slid sideways on the bed, looking at a tilted world.

I felt Nudge get up, heard her run out of the room and down the hall. "Dr. Martinez! Come quick! Something's wrong with Max!"

In a few seconds I felt my mom sit down on the bed, felt her cool hand on my burning forehead.

"Max, honey, what is it?"

Then the room was full of people talking in hushed tones. My mom was stroking my hair away from my face, and I kept wincing as her hand got caught in the tangles.

"Max?" said Nudge. "Iggy made cookies. Here. Just take a bite."

A cookie was pressed against my lips, and I inhaled its chocolatey scent. I opened my eyes all the way, saw what was left of my flock, plus my mom, Dylan, and Jeb, all gathered around me.

"Are you okay?" Nudge looked worried.

"We read the note," said my mom. Then she turned to the others. "Guys, could you give us a minute?" Everyone backed out, and Iggy shut the door behind them.

"You love him so much it feels like you can't go on without him," said my mom.

My startled gaze met her eyes. I had never admitted to anyone, even myself, how much I loved Fang. I bowed my head and gave a tiny nod. Mom took one of my hands and held it.

"You feel like you might die without him," she said.

I tried to swallow, couldn't, and nodded again.

Her hand raised my chin a bit so I could see her clearly.

"Okay," she said gently. "So what are you going to do about it?"

75

FANG WONDERED if Max had seen his note yet. She was going to want to kill him. When—if—he saw her again. He couldn't think about it. That butt Dylan had been right. Fang had to get as far away from the flock as possible. Where, he wasn't sure. Montana? Canada? Papua New Guinea?

But first he had to get some answers at the doctor's house.

And there it was. He'd seen the satellite pictures when Nudge found them. The terrace was wide and empty except for a few lounge chairs. No one was in the pool. Fang dropped lightly onto the terrace.

In the next second, he felt a stinging pinch in his upper

arm. Looking down, he saw a small dart sticking out of his sleeve.

He started to swear, glancing around wildly for the shooter. Then his knees buckled, he swiped the dart away, and the world swirled around him. He saw Dr. Hans walking toward him with a smile, and four uniformed guards rushing over.

"Fang," said Dr. G-H. "I knew it was just a matter of time before either you or Max got here. As you can see, we've been waiting for you."

Fang fell over, whacking his head against the stone terrace but unable to cry out. He weighed a thousand pounds. His hand was too heavy to raise, his eyelids too heavy to keep open. He was drifting into unconsciousness. The last thing he saw was Angel's face looking shocked, her mouth an O of surprise.

Then there was nothing.

76

PAIN.

Fang's head was killing him. He lifted a hand to his temple and felt a large knot there. A scrape on the skin was clotted with blood. There was a large, pulpy lump on the back of his head—that too had dried blood on it. His lip was split and swollen. He couldn't move the fingers of his other hand—they felt like they'd been dipped in gasoline and set on fire.

Breathing hurt so much that Fang knew several of his ribs were broken. He'd felt it before. Where was he? He struggled to remember. What had happened to him?

"Fang?" Angel's voice slowly sank through the haze surrounding him.

"Unggh." Fang tried to swallow. The taste of blood filled

his mouth. His nose was probably broken as well. Finally, with all of his concentration, he managed to pry open one eye. The other eye was swollen shut.

He blinked a couple times. The world was blurry and indistinct. He was aware of bright lights, splotches of darkness, the subdued beeping and hissing of machines. Oh, God—*was he back at the School?*

"School," he managed to croak. A machine started beeping more quickly as fear-fueled adrenaline dumped into his veins like ice water.

"No, no, Fang. This isn't the School. You're okay." Angel's small hand patted his arm. He felt other hands gently but firmly lower his arm to his side, and then a thick, heavy cuff was snapped around his wrist. With great effort he swiveled his head and saw a white-uniformed nurse-type person checking the restraint to make sure it would hold.

His eye searched for Angel. She was standing close to him. Her face looked concerned, but she tried to smile.

"I'm glad you're awake," she said.

"Whass goin' on?" Fang slurred. "Wha happen?"

"You're at Dr. Hans's house, in Malibu," Angel said. "They gave you a...sedative so you wouldn't be upset. It knocked you out, but then you woke up and, like, went crazy. You were smashing everything in sight, threw a chair through a window, you were punching people. They tried to...settle you. But you got hurt." Her voice ended in a whisper and she looked away, her cheeks flaming.

Fang didn't remember any of it. He wondered if it had

really happened that way. Slowly and painfully, he looked at his other arm, which was also restrained. It had an IV drip going into it.

"Whass dat?" he asked.

Angel licked her lips. "It's something to...help you; something—"

"Oh, our guest is awake, is he?"

Fang turned his head, feeling as if concrete bowling balls were shifting inside his skull. Dr. Gunther-Hagen was walking toward him, suit crisp as always.

"Wha the heck is goin' on?" Fang managed.

"Fang, I'm glad you've joined us," said the doctor. "Angel here has made the right decision, to help me in my work. And now you're here too. Fang, by now you're well aware that the world will soon change irrevocably. Not many people will survive. The ones who do will have some sort of adaptive edge that gives them an advantage."

"Leh me up," said Fang, wondering if he *could* sit up. "Gettin' outta here."

"No, not just yet, Fang," said the doctor. He gestured to the drip in Fang's arm. "I've developed a...vaccine, if you will. Given to normal humans, it will enable them to adapt to the new world environment, enhancing their ability to survive. You are already superior, already evolved. I'm incredibly excited to see what effect this will have on you."

Fang glared at the doctor as well as he could with just

one eye. It was hard to make a croak sound menacing, but he tried. "Geh me outta here."

"You have about another ten minutes to go on the IV," said the doctor. "This reactant will combine with your DNA and help spur greater mutations. Your personal evolution will be sped up, made more dramatic."

Oh, great, Fang thought in dismay, subtly testing the strength of his wrist restraints. What would be next? Turning into the Hulk whenever he got upset? That was the problem with mad, megalomaniac scientist types. They loved the idea of the experiment so much that any consequences it had for anyone else seemed unimportant.

"You've observed what a spectacular specimen Dylan is?" the doctor went on. "He's progressing incredibly well. In a very short time, probably days, he'll be decidedly stronger, faster, and more psychologically sophisticated than the flock."

The doctor looked incredibly pleased with himself, practically trembling with excitement and expectation. "This biological material I'm injecting will help *you* catch up to *him*. By that time, of course, Max will already be firmly paired—hmm, perhaps even mated—with Dylan. They will evolve quite brilliantly—together."

Fang became aware of a huge weight on his chest. Nothing was there, but it felt as if an elephant were sitting on him.

The doctor was still talking. "You'll be ready to lead

your own flock by then. Find your own mate. A fit more suited to survival."

Fang started to feel light-headed. "Chest hurts," he whispered. "Can't breathe."

"You're fine," said Dr. G-H confidently. "By the way, do you realize that when Max was here earlier, Fang, she refused my offer to save your life?"

No. He tried to suck in a breath, but the pain in his chest was terrible, and he couldn't move his muscles. His head fell back, and dimly he heard a beeping sound turn into a steady drone. From very far away, Fang heard Angel cry, "Oh, my God! Fang! Doctor Hans!"

77

ANGEL STARED at the heart monitor in horror. A minute ago, its fast, even spikes had showed Fang's normal heart rate of a 140 beats per minute. Now it was a flat line.

Fang lay still on the bed, his good eye slightly open. Angel grabbed his hand.

"Fang! Fang! Wake up!"

"This wasn't supposed to happen!" said Dr. Hans, looking upset. "This drug has been tested on many subjects!"

"But were they normal, to begin with?"

"Yes, mostly...." Dr. Hans trailed off.

The drone of Fang's monitor filled Angel's head. She smacked her hand down on Fang's bed, hard. "Do something!" she yelled at Dr. Hans. "You promised me he wouldn't get hurt! You promised! Do something!"

"It's too late!" said Dr. Hans. "What can I do?"

Whirling, Angel scanned the lab for a phone but spotted nothing. She sped out of the room and leaped up the steps. Still nothing. She raced outside onto the terrace, and once there, closed her eyes. She took a deep breath and pressed her fingers to her temples. *Max, come,* she thought as hard as she could. *Come here now. Fang needs your help. Come now!*

Her eyes popped open and she started scanning the sky, though she knew there was no way Max could be there yet. She didn't even know if Max had heard her—she'd never tried to send a message that far before. There wasn't time for her to fly to the safe house to get Max. All she could do was send thought messages.

Even though it was already too late.

78

MAX, COME. COME HERE NOW. Fang needs your help. Come now!

I froze, balanced on the balcony. I turned to Nudge.

"Did you hear that?"

Nudge shook her head.

"Got a message from Angel," I said. "She said Fang needed my help and to come there now."

"Fang is there?" Nudge asked, unfolding her wings, getting ready to jump off after me. "What happened?"

I paused for just a minute, thinking. I didn't trust Angel, and I sure as heck didn't trust Dr. Nightmare. But if Fang was there...if he really did need my help...

I jumped off the balcony, swearing, and rose into the air. "I can't take the chance," I told Nudge. "Angel alone—I might not go. But I can't take the chance with Fang. I'm going."

I decided to go into warp drive, leaving Nudge and the others, now clustered on the balcony, behind. Pressing my hands flat against the legs of my jeans, I aimed myself in the direction of Malibu. Then I just...shifted into overdrive. Within fifteen seconds, I was streaking through the sky at upward of 250 miles an hour. I'd be there in minutes.

One thing was certain: If something had happened to Fang, and it was Angel's fault, we'd never be in the same flock again. I promised myself that much.

79

DOWN IN THE LAB, Dr. Hans was a blur of activity. He grabbed a hypodermic needle of something and shot it into Fang's IV line. Angel held Fang's hand, watching the machine tensely. Nothing happened.

"Blast!" Dr. Hans shouted. He dashed into the adjacent supply room.

Angel was in a deep state of shock. When her Voice had given her the premonition about Fang, she had just reported it. She hadn't known why, when, or how it would happen. Somehow, she'd thought that telling Max and the others would help it not come true.

Then Dylan had shown up, seeming like the perfect answer: The Voice had said that the best way for everyone to survive was to split the flock up, have two flocks. Max could have Dylan, and Fang could join forces with Angel. Angel would be the leader of her flock, and Fang would be second in command. Having Max and Fang in the same flock was overkill.

Dr. Hans had promised that if Fang came here, everything would be perfect. Then his goons had beaten Fang up, and Dr. Hans had started the IV drip into Fang's arm, telling Angel that Fang was on his way to becoming the most ultimate Fang possible. Lies.

Angel's back straightened—she felt Max coming. Quietly she left Fang's side and went to unlock the lab door. She glanced around but didn't see Dr. Hans's security team. Then she sat again at Fang's side and picked up his hand.

Was she imagining it, or was Fang's hand already becoming cold?

80

I DROPPED DOWN onto the terrace like a bird of prey. As soon as my sneakers thunked onto solid ground, I raced along the terrace until I saw an open door. I rushed through it and immediately down some steps. Somehow, I had seen these steps in the message Angel had sent me—I knew just where to go.

"Fang! Angel?" I yelled, not even trying for stealth. I was storming the castle, not stealing the jewels.

Then through a vast maze of lab tables, metal and glass shelving, gurneys, and all kinds of medical equipment, I saw Fang in a hospital bed, looking beat up, bruised. Way too still and way too pale. Then Angel, rising slowly from beside him like a zombie from the grave and drifting slowly toward me.

"Max, I . . ."

"Angel! What the—" I sprinted across the lab to Fang's side.

I grabbed his hand. It was cold. Unbelievably cold. One eye was open slightly, unseeing.

Fang will be the first to—

I couldn't let myself think it. I couldn't. But he really looked . . . He felt . . .

Just then Dr. Gunther-Hagen appeared from a side room holding some medical supplies. "I see you now regret your decision, Max."

I snarled at the doctor, "What in the name of God happened, you butcher? He looks like he went through a wood chipper!"

"He had a bad reaction to a sedative," said the doctor stiffly. "He was injured."

The solid drone of an alarm sank into my brain, and my gaze snapped to the machinery next to the bed. There was no heartbeat registering.

"He's flatlining!" I shrieked, and grabbed Dr. Hans by the front of his jacket. "Fix him!"

"Why are you so surprised, Max? Your insistence upon being with Fang above all else—well, I warned you quite clearly that no good would come of it. You had the chance to protect all of the ones you love."

Had he killed Fang? Could he have possibly . . . ?

"There's nothing anyone can do. It's too late. I'm sorry."

He had killed Fang. That sentence made absolutely zero

sense to me. It simply did not compute. I shoved the doctor away and turned to Fang.

I wanted to shake Fang's shoulders, splash cold water on his face, tug on his hair. I stared at him. The parts of his face that weren't purple and bruised were not...life colored.

It just didn't make sense.

A remote part of my consciousness registered that the rest of the flock had arrived, were slamming through the lab door. I couldn't even look up. Fang's hand was limp and cold in mine. My brain hadn't kicked into gear yet, had frozen at the entry of the unthinkable thought.

Fang—after everything we'd been through—was...

Gone?

81

THAT SMALL PART of my mind that was still functioning finally made me look up and catch sight of the flock rushing in just as the lab security team flooded the room from another doorway.

The unfriendly familiar face of our old nemesis, Mr. Chu, shocked me out of my daze for a moment.

"Take 'em *out!*" I screeched. "Show no mercy!"

"On it!" Iggy shouted. Even though they knew I couldn't leave Fang's side, I'd never seen the flock look so confident and determined. Maybe it had something to do with the fact that we were in a lab, and we knew our way around labs.

But then again, so did these guys.

Iggy immediately flew across the room, swiping glass

jars and tubes off shelves and tables and then knocking over as many freestanding shelves as he could.

The instant hurricane of thunderous chaos gave the flock an advantage. By the time the men had chosen their targets, the kids had spread to all corners of the room. Grown-ups just think too much.

"Skateboard!" Iggy called to Gazzy. The Gasman used his wings to propel himself toward the high ceiling and grabbed the pipes running across the length of the room. Swinging off like a trapeze artist, he landed on a gurney and went zooming across the lab, knocking over two guards as he went.

Then, an encore performance: Gazzy gurney-boarded back the other way, over the two dazed guards. But this time, the gurney flipped as it caught one of the guards' heads.

Gazzy went flying as though he'd been launched from a cannon, but it was a good shot. He knocked another guard down before he hit the floor.

Nudge had grabbed a metal IV stand and was spinning around with it like a wild whirling dervish. It smashed into a guard's face and he went down, but not a second later, Nudge took a hard punch to the side of her face from another man, her skin splitting under the impact.

The flock's never been shy about using crotch blows, and with a roar, Nudge nailed her assailant, who dropped like a sack of dog food.

"Sorry," Nudge said, kicking him in the head to knock

him out. Then she and Iggy wasted no time rolling him and the other man into nearby empty extralarge lab animal crates.

"Justice!" Nudge cried, slamming a door shut.

There were five guards down, but several to go. Mr. Chu and Dr. Hans were still on the loose as well. It could have easily been a lost battle without the secret weapon. Dylan.

The youngest but most powerful bird kid held nothing back as he took out one attacker after another. He was coldly furious and determined—almost scary. Everything about his quiet, easygoing demeanor had disappeared. Now his fists slammed into faces, he spun into kicks that had taken us years to master. His blows knocked grown men off their feet; his roundhouse kick shot a guard eight feet back, into a wall.

Total had been right: He was a fighting machine.

Meanwhile, Dr. Hans was watching everything from a safe corner, a scientist unemotionally observing his lab animals. But no one had noticed that Angel was missing from the fray. She now dashed out of the supply room clutching six or seven different-sized containers.

"Gazzy! What's good here?" It was flock shorthand for: *Is there anything you can make blow up here?*

Gazzy had just recovered from his cannon-fire episode. He ran over and scanned faster than a computer. "No explosives, but there's some pretty acidic stuff," he determined, pulling three canisters aside. "Some of this is gonna hurt super bad."

"Not so fast, children." The impeccably dressed Mr. Chu—who'd been cowering under a lab table to avoid the fight, or to avoid ruining his suit—now appeared at their side.

"Chu!" Gazzy gasped.

"You know *a lot* about toxic chemicals, if I remember, sir," Angel said, stalling. "Maybe you can help us."

At that moment, with a perfect swan dive from the suspended pipes, Iggy crashed into Mr. Chu, knocking him onto the floor. The breath left Mr. Chu's body in a sharp *oof!* Iggy got his hands around Mr. Chu's neck and started twisting.

"Oh, my God!" Gazzy shouted a few seconds later. Angel's mouth was open in horror.

Mr. Chu's face *had come off in Iggy's hands,* and Iggy was now holding it like a huge, disgusting face glove.

"What happened?" Iggy cried.

Nudge hurried to his side. There, on the ground, with Mr. Chu's body, was the head of a...freak? His boyish, round face was flat, green, and scaly, and he had a kid's wide eyes.

"Jeezum pete," Nudge breathed.

"Don't kill me," pleaded the freak.

"Let Robert up," ordered Dr. Death from the corner.

"Robert?" Iggy almost shrieked. "He's *green!*"

"Watch it, guys!" Dylan warned. Some of the men who'd been down earlier were back up and staggering toward them. They moved just slowly enough to allow Angel,

Nudge, and Gazzy to pry open the containers and start dousing the men with chemical agents that kids should never have access to.

"Incapacitate them," Dylan ordered, catching his breath. "I've got to get the doctor."

82

THE FIGHT UNFOLDED like background noise. White noise. In the foreground, even with his ghastly pale face looking dead in my hands, my fingers clenching his ragged hair, all I could see was random images of Fang, *not dead*.

Fang telling me stupid fart jokes from the dog crate next to mine at the School, trying to make me laugh.

Fang asleep at Jeb's old house, and me jumping wildly on his bed to wake him up. Him pretending to be asleep. Me laughing when I "accidentally" kicked him where it counts. Him dumping me off the bed.

Fang gagging on my first attempt at cooking dinner after Jeb disappeared. Him spitting out the mac and cheese. Me dumping the rest of the bowl on him in response.

Fang on the beach, that first time he was badly injured. Me realizing how I felt about him.

Fang kissing me. So close I couldn't even see his dark eyes anymore. The first time. The second time. The third.

I could remember each and every one of them. Would always remember them.

Fang.

Not.

Dead.

83

THEN A COUPLE of my nerves started firing again, and my muscles unfroze.

"Fang! Come back!" I started pulling his hair. Shaking his head and shoulders. Hard. "Wake up! Snap out of it! You stupid jerk! I am going to kill you if you die on me!"

I put my mouth up to his ear. "Did you *hear me?*" I was yelling right into it. "Dying is *not* on the agenda! Not part of my plan!"

That wasn't working. I pounded on his chest. "Get *up!* After everything we've been through, are you going to give up now? Are you that much of a wuss? We need you, you butthead! *I* need you. I—I *love* you, Fang."

I was choking on dry sobs now. "Did you *hear* that?

Why I didn't I tell you before? You can't die before I tell you that. You *can't!*"

Gulping, I looked around wildly, as if I would see something marked "Second chances. Use sparingly." All I saw were a bunch of unconscious guards, bloody bird kids, and a lizard boy.

And a large hypodermic needle, on the stand holding medical equipment next to Fang's bed. The tube was marked "Adrenaline. Dangerous."

I reached for it. I had seen this movie once—

"I tried that!" said Dr. Disaster, who was tightly in Dylan's grip. "Don't you think I tried that? I shot it into his IV! It did nothing!"

In a split second I grabbed the hypo, whirled, and sank the needle deep into Fang's chest, directly into his heart. I pressed the plunger home, emptying its entire contents. If he had any chance at all, this was it. And if it wouldn't save his life, then it would surely end it once and for all, right now.

Being a leader means you have to make life-or-death decisions sometimes. And I made this one.

84

TIME BECAME ELASTIC, stretching out endlessly. Each second seemed to take hours. Everyone was moving in slow motion, all blurry, all dreamy. I couldn't understand what they were saying. I got an impression of Iggy and Gazzy holding Robert down, trying to pull off his new head, without success. I saw Nudge and Angel hugging. Angel was crying.

One by one they turned to look at me and Fang, concern and pain on their faces.

I looked down at Fang, at that smooth, tan place on his neck where his pulse should have been beating. I squeezed his cold hand hard, willing him to squeeze back. I dropped my head to his chest and closed my eyes so I wouldn't have to see the machine flatlining in front of me.

Fang, come on, I thought. *You promised you would never leave me. You promised.* I gulped again, hearing nothing, feeling nothing under my ear. *This can't be, can't be, can't be....Oh, God, help me, help me....*

My mind was starting to completely shut down in order not to feel this pain, when I heard a *beep*.

Then another *beep*.

Then I felt Fang's chest rise as he gasped in a breath, and I felt his heart beat, right under my cheek.

I bolted upright, staring at his face. His mouth opened. His good eye widened. I grabbed his hand in both of mine and clasped it hard against my chest. I couldn't say anything, could only stare at that poor, battered face I loved so much.

Fang blinked hazily and breathed in again. His gaze fell on me, and I must have looked wild with panic and misery.

"Fang?" I gasped.

He blinked, tried to swallow. "'Ssup?" he said groggily.

I'm pretty much of the stoical school of emotiveness, but everything I was feeling burst through me like a flood through a dam. I dropped my head back onto his chest, my arms around him, and sobbed.

85

"LET ME GO! I *command* you!" I heard Dr. Gunther-Hagen shout. "Have you lost your mind? Have you forgotten who I am?" I looked around and saw Dylan, flecked with blood and sporting a black eye, grasping the doctor from behind. He was staring at the doctor with fury, even hatred.

"I think you've forgotten who *I* am," Dylan countered. "That is, not a robot. Someone with a mind of his own."

"But you—you owe me your *life!*" Dr. G-H stammered.

"I'm not sure I want this life," Dylan said sadly. And he looked at me and Fang.

The doctor's eyes got even wider as he became fully aware of Fang's regained consciousness. "This doesn't make sense!"

"*You* don't make sense!" I bit out through my tears.

"We're not just test subjects! We're not just for experimenting! You people never learn!"

"I see it all clearly now," Dylan said in an oddly flat, quiet voice. "I see what you are. I see what you made me. And I see what I'll become." He looked over at another gurney a few yards away from him. "Iggy, can you help me with this? Grab his legs."

Iggy and Dylan lifted the struggling doctor onto the gurney. "Gazzy, Nudge, Angel, you too. We need help strapping him down."

I was dumbfounded as I watched my flock restrain this evil genius on a gurney. As had been done to us so many times in our lives.

But the next thing surprised me even more.

Dylan picked up another fully loaded giant hypo from the tray next to Fang's bed. "This should do nicely." He readied the needle like a trained nurse. It was obvious that he'd been raised on injections.

Dr. Gunther-Hagen craned his head to look around at his lab, now destroyed; his guards, now useless; his subject Fang, now saved. And his master creation, Dylan, who looked as though he wanted to kill him.

"That's what I call giving someone a taste of their own medicine," Gazzy whispered.

"You don't know what you're doing, Dylan," the doctor said.

"Let's pin his arm down, please," Dylan directed quietly, and placed the tip of the needle on the vein. He was like a beautiful, powerful avenging angel.

And yet—he was...scary.

Nudge bit her lip. Angel looked confused. Iggy didn't look anything.

I suddenly had a flash of myself saying something—it seemed like years ago. *Someday we might have only a few seconds to figure out the meaning of life.*

"Oh, God, Dylan—don't," I found myself pleading. "It's just—enough. Enough already."

Dylan stopped. Just like that. "Okay, Max."

He looked at me, then at Fang, then at the doctor.

Then he plunged the needle into his own arm.

EPILOGUE

EPILOGUE

AFTER EVERYTHING, we've come to this, I thought.

I felt weird in my fancy dress, but even I had to admit it was gorgeous. Someone had come to the house this morning and fixed all of our hair—Angel's golden halo of curls had never looked so perfect. Or so clean. Nudge looked even more like a teen model than usual, with her long, honey-streaked brown ringlets falling in perfect array around her shoulders. They were wearing matching dresses of russet silk. I glanced down at my cream-colored one, praying that I didn't get dirt or blood on it before this was all over.

We carried flowers, bouquets of wildflowers that we'd picked this morning among the beautiful Colorado hills.

Nudge came up and stood next to me in the tent,

peeking out through the door slit. It was a stunning afternoon, and in front of us, under a natural arch of trees, was a long red carpet with white chairs arranged on either side. Nudge smiled up at me.

"You've never looked more beautiful," she said, and I gave a nervous grin. My hair was pulled back away from my face, and I had a little crown of flowers woven into it. I too was exceedingly clean.

Our various bruises and scrapes had healed completely, and Fang's injuries were only a bad memory—as was Dylan's pseudo suicide attempt. He'd suffered no ill consequences of the injection thus far. Plus, we hadn't seen Dr. Gunther-Hagen again. We'd rolled him kicking and screaming into a giant lab cold-storage room before splitting that day, but I was sure one of his posse would revive and let the doc out of his icebox before he turned into a Popsicle.

"Is that the justice of the peace?" Nudge whispered.

"Yeah. She's a friend of my mom's." I saw my mom and my half sister, Ella, sitting in the second row, looking back to see us. Jeb and Dylan were in the next row, and a bunch of our friends from CSM. Dylan had really surprised me, down in Dr. G-H's lair. I was gonna keep an eye on him.

"There's the music," said Angel.

"Okay, you're up," I said. The two of us really hadn't hashed things out. I knew we'd have to, if the flock was going to survive. But not today.

Angel slipped through the tent door. Everyone oohed

and aahed at how pretty she was. She walked slowly down the red carpet, strewing white rose petals everywhere. Deceptively innocent, I thought. But at the same time it was comforting to see her looking so much like my old Angel. Even though we hadn't fully made amends for all that had happened between us, I decided to suck it up and enjoy the rush of everything that was happening today.

"Your turn," I told Nudge. She gave me one last smile, then headed down the red carpet slowly, walking in time to the music. I peered out and saw Gazzy step forward, right in front of the justice of the peace. He took Angel's arm and they walked a few paces, then separated and stood on either side of the decorated podium.

I waited until Nudge was halfway down the aisle, then I left the tent, hoping I didn't throw up from tension. Everyone's heads turned toward me, and I heard excited whispers ripple through the small crowd. I tried to smile, but I was so nervous I could manage only a sickly grin. Ahead of me, Iggy stepped out unerringly and took Nudge's arm. They walked a few paces, then separated, like Angel and Gazzy.

Then I could see Fang. His dark eyes seemed to burn as they locked on me. I tried to swallow and couldn't. I was holding my bouquet so tightly I was about to snap all the stems. Everyone else faded away, and I had eyes only for Fang. His black hair had been cut, somewhat. He wore a midnight-blue suit and an actual tie that he'd probably already figured out fifteen ways to kill someone with.

It seemed to take forever, but I finally made it up to Fang without tripping on my impractical fancy shoes. He held out his arm and I took it, staring into his eyes. We walked up to the justice of the peace...and separated, each standing on our own side.

Then everyone really craned their heads around to see Akila stepping lightly from the tent. A wreath of flowers like mine rested between her pointed ears, with lisianthus picking up the blue of her intelligent eyes.

She walked majestically down the aisle, just as my mom had practiced with her.

As she stopped in front of the justice of the peace, Total stepped over to join her. He was wearing a russet-colored bow tie, and his black fur shone. Even his black wings, which he held out proudly, looked perfectly groomed.

Total grinned at me, and I smiled back at him. It didn't matter that he was shorter than Akila, that she outweighed him by sixty pounds. It didn't matter that he was a mutant, and she was 100 percent glorious purebred. The way they looked at each other would have brought a tear to my eye, if I were susceptible to that kind of thing.

Total knew how difficult their future would be. He could fly on his own—he was as capable as we were of jumping up and going somewhere at a moment's notice. Akila was stuck with more traditional means of travel. Total could talk to us, express his wants and needs (lord, could he), whereas he had to interpret Akila for us.

But they had decided to stick together, despite the odds.

Total had fastened on to Akila as being the perfect match for him the moment he had first seen her. He hadn't given up. And now they were declaring their vows in front of everyone they cared about.

My mind wandered as the justice of the peace began the ceremony. I heard Total say, "I do," in a voice quavering with emotion. Next to him, Akila nodded that she did too.

I couldn't help looking over at Fang, unbearably handsome, the afternoon sun turning his skin to a warm gold. He was already looking at me, and I shivered at the expression on his face. In his eyes I saw the promise of *our* future together. A future full of danger, excitement, persecution, thrilling victories, and lessons learned—some easy, some hard.

And every bit of it would be okay. Because we would be together.

THE OTHER EPILOGUE

AS IT TURNED OUT, that assumption was wrong.

After the reception, which was pretty much the funnest party I'd ever been to, especially since I didn't have to put it together or clean up afterward, we headed back to our current safe house. Fang had gone back about an hour before but had insisted I stay and eat cake and party down with my funky self.

So I did, in my fancy dress and fancy shoes and fancy hair, and I couldn't help marveling at the fact that it wasn't all that long ago that we were sleeping in subway tunnels in New York, and it probably wouldn't be all that long before some similar change in our circumstances took place.

But tonight was fabulous, and I was surrounded by my favorite people, and I kept thinking of funny things to tell

Fang, like how Total looked with white frosting all over his face.

So Nudge and I flew back, followed by Angel, Gazzy, and Iggy. I was thankful that I could usually wear jeans or sweats. Flying in a dress is not a picnic. Talk about vulnerable.

We landed lightly on our back deck. Inside, a few lights were on. I kicked off my fashionable, uncomfortable shoes and went to find Fang. I'd brought him a piece of cake, and though it was a teensy bit squooshed, I was sure it'd taste okay.

I headed down the hall and tapped on the closed door of the boys' room. No answer. Had he already fallen asleep?

I opened the door a bit and peered in. It was dark.

"Fang?"

I flicked on the light. The room was empty; his bed was still made. The bathroom was next door, and it too was dark and empty.

"Fang?" I called louder. "We're home!"

I headed out to ask the others if they'd seen him, and that was when I saw the note.

It was propped on the dresser, by the door—a white envelope with my name written on it in Fang's spiky handwriting.

My heart dropped somewhere around my stomach, and my skin went cold, as if I'd stepped into a freezer. Slowly I reached out and picked up the envelope. I opened the flap and pulled out a sheet of paper.

"Max? What are you doing? We're gonna take a couple more photos," said Nudge, swinging around the door. "Since we probably won't all be clean at the same time ever again."

I swallowed. "Is Fang out there with you guys?"

"No—he's not in here?"

"No. I found this." I showed her the note, and her eyes went wide.

"What is it?" Her voice was hushed and solemn.

Breathing shallowly, I unfolded the paper. I didn't want to read it—like, if I didn't read it, it would make it not be true.

But I was not a coward. Even about this. So I started reading aloud.

Dear Max—
You looked so beautiful today. I'm going to remember what you looked like forever.

Nudge put her hand over her mouth.

And I hope you remember me the same way—clean, ha-ha. I'm glad our last time together was happy.

But I'm leaving tonight, leaving the flock, and this time it's for good. I don't know if I'll ever see any of you again. The thing is, Max, that everyone is a little bit right. Added up all together, it makes this one big right.

Dylan's a little bit right about how my being here might be putting the rest of you in danger. The threat might have been just about Dr. Hans, but we don't know

305

that for sure. Angel is a little bit right about how splitting up the flock will help all of us survive. And the rest of the flock is a little bit right about how when you and I are together, we're focused on each other—we can't help it.

The thing is, Maximum, I love you. I can't help but be focused on you when we're together. If you're in the room, I want to be next to you. If you're gone, I think about you. You're who I want to talk to. In a fight, I want you at my back. When we're together, the sun is shining. When we're apart, everything is in shades of gray.

I hope you'll forgive me someday for turning our worlds into shades of gray—at least for a while.

I stopped for a moment, trying to breathe. The others had trickled down the hall to see what we were doing, and they were all crowded around Nudge, their faces shocked.

You're not at your best when you're focused on me. I mean, you're at your best Maxness, but not your best leaderness. I mostly need Maxness. The flock mostly needs leaderness. And Angel, if you're listening to this, it ain't you, sweetie. Not yet.

I glanced at Angel, and her cheeks flushed.

At least for a couple more years, the flock needs a leader to survive, no matter how capable everyone thinks he or she is. The truth is that they do need a leader, and the truth is that you are the best leader. It's one of the things I love about you.

But the more I thought about it, the more sure I got that this is the right thing to do. Maybe not for you, or for me, but for all of us together, our flock.

Please don't try to find me. This is the hardest thing I've ever done in my life, besides wearing that suit today, and seeing you again will only make it harder. You'd ask me to come back, and I would, because I can't say no to you. But all the same problems would still be there, and I'd end up leaving again, and then we'd have to go through this all over again.

Please make us only go through this once.

My throat was closing up, my voice becoming raspy. I could think of *lots* of times he'd told me no. Nudge edged her hand into the crook of my arm, holding on as if we both needed support.

I love you. I love your smile, your snarl, your grin, your face when you're sleeping. I love your hair streaming out behind you as we fly, with the sunlight making it shine, if it doesn't have too much mud or blood in it. I love seeing your wings spreading out, white and brown and tan and speckled, and the tiny, downy feathers right at the top of your shoulders. I love your eyes, whether they're cold or calculating or suspicious or laughing or warm, like when you look at me.

I started crying, like a big doofus. I couldn't believe this. I wiped my tears away with the sleeve of my fancy dress.

You're the best warrior I know, the best leader. You're the most comforting mom we've ever had. You're the biggest goofball, the worst driver, and a truly lousy cook. You've kept us safe and provided for us, in good times and bad. You're my best friend, my first and only love, and the most beautiful girl I've ever seen, with wings or without.

Now everyone was crying, even Iggy. We were all sniffing and wiping our faces, and I knew I was right: Reading this out loud meant it had really happened, was really happening. To all of us, not just to me.

Tell you what, sweetie: If in twenty years we haven't expired yet, and the world is still more or less in one piece, I'll meet you at the top of that cliff where we first met the hawks and learned to fly with them. You know the one. Twenty years from today, if I'm alive, I'll be there, waiting for you. You can bet on it.

Good-bye, my love.

Fang

P.S. Tell everyone I sure will miss them.

We were all silent. The letter was wet with my tears, making some of the words run. Fang was usually, well, *reserved* is a nice word for it. But this letter had poured out a lifetime's worth of love. I felt numb, like someone had just whapped my head hard.

"I can't believe it," said Gazzy.

"That butthead," said Iggy.

"This is my fault," said Angel, her shoulders hunching with sobs.

"No," I told her. "You've done a lot of asinine things, but this is not your fault."

I felt very old and very tired. Total and Akila's wedding seemed as if it had happened a year ago. Nudge put her head on my shoulder. I set the letter down and put my arms around her.

Tears were dripping onto my dress, but I wasn't making any sound. There was no sound that could express this kind of pain.

I didn't want to move, didn't want to do anything. Fang was not waiting for me out in the living room. Tomorrow morning, when I woke up, Fang would still be gone.

I feel like I'm going to HURL. Which, even if I wanted to do, I couldn't do, because I haven't eaten. I can't even drag myself out of my room. And while I'd be able to muster the strength to roundhouse Fang until he begged for MERCY, I'd be mush around an Eraser. In fact, all I want to flipping do is lie on this bed with our old laptop and catch up on my Hulu. Apparently, being heartbroken is not leverage enough to get Nudge to give up the NEW computer, so I'm stuck with the old laptop.

But what to my wondering eyes should appear, the very moment I turn the thing on?

What did that stupid deserting crap-bag ex-boyfriend, ex-best friend with the most perfect stupid hair do? He DIDN'T delete his crap off the desktop before he fled my life and left me all alone. That's what he did.

FangStuff

Do I open it?
Do I open it?
Of course I freaking open it!!!!!!

MAX	
Pro	Con
Good leader	Drill sergeant
Could possibly kill anyone/thing with bare hands	Could possibly kill me with bare hands
Can save the world	Has to save the world
Pretty	Doesn't shower
Smart	Knows it all
Good taste in music	Can't sing. At all.
Likes me	Hot for Dylan
Eats as much as I do	Burps like a trucker
Believes in me	Skeptical of EVERYONE else
Needs me sometimes	Doesn't need me sometimes
Thinks with her heart	Reacts with her heart
Keeps me on my game	Stubborn doesn't cover it
Nice lips	Bony toes
Can act like she's my mom	Eew
Wants to make the world a better place	Takes on too much
Could stay with her forever	Distraction from what we need to do

Chad, Africa

Hot, Hungry, and Thankful Not to Have HIV O'clock

Here we are in Africa, where the focus is not on us and our problems. It's on the crippling injustice in the world. The GDP ("gross domestic product"—don't ask me; just look it up!) of Chad is 16.1 *billion* dollars. The GDP of the USA is 14.3 *trillion* dollars. Chew on that.

It's pretty overwhelming. What can I, in the tiny scope of one life, possibly do to make a lasting and large change in the world? I'm a bird kid and a borderline celebrity at this point...but still, I'm just a drop in the bucket.

I'm down tonight, so here I am blithering on like Nudge. Max is asleep, and so is everyone else. Strange. We bird kids don't take sleep for granted, you know? Occasionally things chill out ... but they never really chill out. We just forget how crazy everything is....

Okay. The bottom line is that what Angel said scared the bejeezy out of me. There. I said it.

'Cause I'm going to die *"first"* and *"soon."*

I could string that sinister little mind-reading Shirley Temple up by her pinafores for her total lack of elaboration. Except Max about beat me to it.

I'm lucky. Somehow I got the "unable to visually emote" genetic modification. Because inside, when Angel said that, my blood froze and my bird bones ached.

So what's her prediction worth anyway? Where does it come from? From a Voice, like Max's? Doesn't mean it's right. We only assume it's always going to be right, because it has the power to invade her brain and be so FLIPPING CREEPY. But creepy doesn't mean all-powerful.

It's like I'm trying to talk myself out of this. Of course we're going to die. And it's probably going to be sooner rather than later. And it's not going to be fun. Look at the life we lead.

Twelve hours ago were we not being shot at by crazy guys on camels with semiautomatic weapons?

That's what I thought.

Crap.

Sigh.

Fly on,
Fang

I'm Not Telling, Colorado

The Day Before Our Birthday O'clock

So, we have on *The Gift List*:

Iggy—Gory, gooey, blood-spattering audiobook on CD. **CHECK**

Nudge—584,395,004,981 fashion magazines. **CHECK**

Gazzy—Illustrated history of blowing crap up for eons. **CHECK CHECK**

Angel—Angel? A camera, a great gift for a smart, creative kid. **CHECK**

Max—...

Max—...Roses? They die. **LAME**

Max—...Poetry? And she beats me up....**OW**

Max—...Jewelry?...Pretty?...Can't be used (easily) as a weapon?

What could possibly be right for Max? That girl is fiercer than a rattlesnake. Pft. In fact, the first few times we kissed, I thought she was one. That girl was a regular old teeth-banger. (And they call *me* Fang.) Thank goodness she was genetically engineered to have good teeth. If she had braces, my gums would have been ground beef. But I wouldn't care if she was the worst teeth-banger in a pool of every high school student on the planet. In fact, I like her more because of it.

Man, I don't know. I'm really not sure. The secret to gifts is...? Right, ask me, the fifteen-year-old (tomorrow) bird man. I know *everything* about gift giving. I learned in charm school.

I think the secret to a great gift is that it should be personal. It has to prove that you know and care about someone enough to know what she'd love. And I'm so dead.

I hope I made the right choice. That ring, I want it to mean something.

She's going to think I'm the corniest guy on the planet.

Fly on,
Fang

Las Vegas, Nevada

We Won the Jackpot—If by Jackpot You Mean You're Willing to Deal with Exile—O'clock

Welcome to the funhouse, Faxness. You've arrived in fabulous Las Vegas, otherwise known as the most genetically modified city on the planet. Looks can be deceiving, folks. Unnatural bliss, ladies and gentlemen, unnatural, impossible bliss.

Last night Max and I arrived in Vacationland—and promptly proceeded to stuff as many corn nuts, funnel cakes, spumoni cones, sushi rolls, heroes, falafels, cheese steaks, burritos, and wasabi peas into our mouths as we could find.

So romantic, I know. But it was, though. It was awesome. It was about seventy-five degrees and crisp and dry out. It was perfect, walking down the streets, licking spumoni. The city was lit up like neon heaven.

But it was sad too. I thought that by going somewhere we'd blend in, we'd be able to escape. But the thing about Vegas is that it's impossible, even for one second, to forget that this city is totally false. There's even a *fake Paris*.

It reminds me that being here in Vacationland with Max, just being alone together doing outrageous fun things, that's false too.

Or short-lived, anyway. How long did it take for Dr. Hagen-Doodie to find us? Less than twenty-four hours? Exactly.

I can see it in Max's eyes—we're going to last about as long in Vacationland as we did in Max School.

Surprise! Life isn't Las Vegas. Or Disney World. For us bird kids, maybe it's more like Death Valley.

Fly on,
Fang

Dylan,

I don't think I've ever hated anyone more than I hate you. Maybe evil scientists. But they don't count. The way I feel about you is different. I can't control it. I don't care that you're a test-tube mutant and can't help it. I don't care if you're the nicest and smartest dude in the universe and can sing better than Bono. I want Max to be mine. You have no right to touch her. I don't care how the wack-job whitecoats programmed you. I've been by her side practically since the day she was born.

But I can't be around. My anger toward you is getting in the way. Clouding my decisions. I don't know what is the right thing to do. And this thing with Max...it's a thing with you too.

Yo,
I have no choice but to respond to this. Why? Because it's funny. Never underestimate the power of funny. It moves mountains.

From Jess:
FANG.
I've commented your blog with my questions for THREE YEARS. You answer other people's STUPID questions but not MINE. YOU REALLY ASKED FOR IT, BUDDY. I'm just gonna comment with this until you answer at least one of my questions.

DO YOU HAVE A JAMAICAN ACCENT?
No, mon.

DO YOU MOLT?
Gross.

WHAT'S YOUR STAR SIGN?
Don't know. "Angel, what's my star sign?" She says Scorpio.

HAVE YOU TOLD JEB I LOVE HIM YET?
No.

DOES NOT HAVING A POWER MAKE YOU ANGRY?
Well, that's not really true....

DO YOU KNOW HOW TO DO THE SOULJA BOY?
Can you see me doing the Soulja Boy?

DOES IGGY KNOW HOW TO DO THE SOULJA BOY?
Gazzy does.

DO YOU USE HAIR PRODUCTS?
No. Again, no.

DO YOU USE PRODUCTS ON YOUR FEATHERS?
I don't know that they make bird kid feather products yet.

WHAT'S YOUR FAVORITE MOVIE?
There are a bunch.

WHAT'S YOUR FAVORITE SONG?
I don't have favorites. They're too polarizing.

WHAT'S YOUR FAVORITE SMELL?
Max, when she showers.

DO THESE QUESTIONS MAKE YOU ANGRY?
Not really.

IF I CAME UP TO YOU IN A STREET AND HUGGED YOU,
WOULD YOU KILL ME?
You might get kicked. But I'm used to people wanting me
dead, so.

DO YOU SECRETLY WANT TO BE HUGGED?
Doesn't everybody?

ARE YOU GOING EMO 'CAUSE ANGEL IS STEALING
EVERYONE'S POWERS (INCLUDING YOURS)?
Not the emo thing again.

WHAT'S YOUR FAVORITE FOOD?
Anything hot and delicious and brought to me by Iggy.

WHAT DID YOU HAVE FOR BREAKFAST THIS MORNING?
Three eggs, over easy. Bacon. More bacon. Toast.

DID YOU EVEN HAVE BREAKFAST THIS MORNING?
See above.

DID YOU DIE INSIDE WHEN MAX CHOSE ARI OVER YOU?
Dudes don't die inside.

DO YOU LIKE MAX?
Duh.

DO YOU LIKE ME?
I think you're funny.

DOES IGGY LIKE ME?
Sure.

DO YOU WRITE DEPRESSING POETRY?
No.

IS IT ABOUT MAX?
Ahh. No.

IS IT ABOUT ARI?
Why do you assume I write depressing poetry?

IS IT ABOUT JEB?
Ahh.

ARE YOU GOING TO BLOCK THIS COMMENT?
Clearly, no.

WHAT ARE YOU WEARING?
A Dirty Projectors T-shirt. Jeans.

DO YOU WEAR BOXERS OR BRIEFS?
No freaking comment.

DO YOU FIND THIS COMMENT PERSONAL?
Could I not find that comment personal?

DO YOU WEAR SUNGLASSES?
Yes, cheap ones.

DO YOU WEAR YOUR SUNGLASSES AT NIGHT?
That would make it hard to see.

DO YOU SMOKE APPLES, LIKE US?
Huh?

DO YOU PREFER BLONDES OR BRUNETTES?
Whatever.

DO YOU LIKE VAMPIRES OR WEREWOLVES?
Fanged creatures rock.

ARE YOU GAY AND JUST PRETENDING TO BE STRAIGHT BY
KISSING LISSA?
Uhh…

WERE YOU EXPERIMENTING WITH YOUR SEXUALITY?
Uhh…

WOULD YOU TELL US IF YOU WERE GAY?
Yes.

DO YOU SECRETLY LIKE IT WHEN PEOPLE CALL YOU EMO?
No.

ARE YOU EMO?
Whatever.

DO YOU LIKE EGGS?
Yes. I had them for breakfast.

DO YOU LIKE EATING THINGS?
I love eating. I list it as a hobby.

DO YOU SECRETLY THINK YOU'RE THE SEXIEST PERSON IN THE
WHOLE WORLD?
Do you secretly think I'm the sexiest person in the whole
world?

DO YOU EVER HAVE DIRTY THOUGHTS ABOUT MAX?
Eeek!

HAS ANGEL EVER READ YOUR MIND WHEN YOU WERE
HAVING DIRTY THOUGHTS ABOUT MAX AND GONE "OMG"
AND YOU WERE LIKE "D:"?
hahahahahahahahahahah

DO YOU LIKE SPONGEBOB?
He's okay, I guess.

DO YOU EVER HAVE DIRTY THOUGHTS ABOUT SPONGEBOB?
Definitely.

CAN YOU COOK?
Iggy cooks.

DO YOU LIKE TO COOK?
I like to eat.

ARE YOU, LIKE, A HOUSEWIFE?
How on earth could I be like a housewife?

DO YOU SECRETLY HAVE INNER TURMOIL?
Isn't it obvious?

DO YOU WANT TO BE UNDA DA SEA?
I'm unda da stars.

DO YOU THINK IT'S NOT TOO LATE, IT'S NEVER TOO LATE?
Sure.

WHERE DID YOU LEARN TO PLAY POKER?
TV.

DO YOU HAVE A GOOD POKER FACE?
Totally.

OF COURSE YOU HAVE A GOOD POKER FACE. DOES IGGY
HAVE A GOOD POKER FACE?
Yes.

CAN HE EVEN PLAY POKER?
Iggy beats me sometimes.

DO YOU LIKE POKING PEOPLE, HARD?
Not really.

ARE YOU FANGALICIOUS?
I could never be as fangalicious as you'd want me to be.

Fly on,
Fang

Dear Max—
You looked so beautiful today. I'm going to remember what you looked like forever. And I hope you remember me the same way—clean, ha-ha. I'm glad our last time together was happy.

But I'm leaving tonight, leaving the flock, and this time it's for good. I don't know if I'll ever see any of you again. The thing is, Max, that everyone is a little bit right. Added up all together, it makes this one big right.

Dylan's a little bit right about how my being here might be putting the rest of you in danger. The threat might have been just about Dr. Hans, but we don't know that for sure. Angel is a little bit right about how splitting up the flock will help all of us survive. And the rest of the flock is a little bit right about how when you and I are together, we're focused on each other—we can't help it.

~~Jeb and Dr. Hans are even a little bit right. Jeb with his weird way of showing up at the most random times—with the most random but kinda relevant advice. Dr. Hans about mutants being the way of the future and about how we should learn about ourselves. Not that I want to be injected with anything, ever. But the world is changing, and there are others of us out there. I can't tell you how I know. But I do. And how we save the world, that's a huge question. It's complicated, Max. It's so very large.~~

The thing is, Maximum, I love you. I can't help but be focused on you when we're together. If you're in the room, I want to be next to you. If you're gone, I think about you. You're who I want to talk to. In a fight, I want you at my back. When we're together, the sun is shining. When we're apart, everything is in shades of gray.

I hope you'll forgive me someday for turning our worlds into shades of gray—at least for a while. ~~It's not right that we're together. There are too many risks and too many reasons why not. I must not be selfish.~~

You're not at your best when you're focused on me. I mean, you're at your best Maxness, but not your best leaderness. I mostly need Maxness. The flock mostly needs leaderness. And Angel, if you're listening to this, it ain't you, sweetie. Not yet.

At least for a couple more years, the flock needs a leader to survive, no matter how capable everyone thinks he or she is. The truth is that they do need a leader, and the truth is that you are the best leader. ~~I've learned everything from you.~~ It's one of the things I love about you.

But the more I thought about it, the more sure I got that this is the right thing to do. Maybe not for you, or for me, but for all of us together, our flock.

~~I know where I'm going, but~~ please don't try to find me. This is the hardest thing I've ever done in my life, besides wearing that suit today, and seeing you again will only make it harder. ~~I don't know how I'm going to manage to do what you do all by myself. If I were to see you again,~~ you'd ask me to come back, and I would, because I can't say no to you. But all the same problems would still be there, and I'd end up leaving again, and then we'd have to go through this all over again.

Please make us go through this only once. ~~We must stand strong, alone and apart.~~

I love you. I love your smile, your snarl, your grin, your face when you're sleeping. I love your hair streaming out behind you as we fly, with the sunlight making it shine, if it doesn't have too much mud or blood in it. I love seeing your wings spreading out, white and brown and tan and speckled, and the tiny, downy feathers right at the top of your shoulders. I love your eyes, whether they're cold or calculating or suspicious or laughing or warm, like when you look at me.

You're the best warrior I know, the best leader. You're the most comforting mom we've ever had. You're the biggest goofball, the worst driver, and a truly lousy cook. You've kept us safe and provided for us, in good times and bad. You're my best friend, my first and only love, and the most beautiful girl I've ever seen, with wings or without.

Tell you what, sweetie: If ~~I accomplish what I've set out to do and~~ in twenty years we haven't expired yet, and the world is still more or less in one piece, I'll meet you at the top of that cliff where we first met the hawks and learned to fly with them. You know the one. Twenty years from today, if I'm alive, I'll be there, waiting for you. You can bet on it.

Good-bye, my love.

Fang

P.S. Tell everyone I sure will miss them.

~~P.P.S. Tell Dylan he was right. He belongs with us.~~

NEEDED: GEN 77 and/or HUMAN-ANIMAL HYBRIDS

Yo,

Feel like you don't fit in? Do you know that you're different? Can you do things no one else can? If you know what I'm talking about, the world is changing and I need your help.

Tell me your skills and send me your coordinates. I'll be in touch.

http://www.max-dan-wiz.com/profile/Fang4

Fly on,

Fang

ANNOUNCING THE
WINNER
OF THE ΜΑΧΙΜΩΜ RIDE WRITING CONTEST!

Desperate to find out what happened when Max took
Dylan on his first flying lesson in *FANG*?
Maximum Ride fans between ages 13 and 18 took a stab
at writing an outline and the "missing chapter" between
Chapters 35 and 36. The contest ran in Spring 2010.

AND HERE IS THE WINNING ENTRY FROM:
Taylor R. from California

CONGRATULATIONS!

CHAPTER 35½ OUTLINE

   I. Dylan attempts to fly onto the roof of the house.

     A. Dylan falls at first.

     B. Max shows Dylan how to fly to the roof.

     C. Dylan succeeds in flying up.

  II. Max pushes Dylan off the roof.

 III. Dylan succeeds in flying, and Max joins him on a flight over the canyon.

 IV. Max and Dylan accidentally brush wings.

  V. The two share a tender moment.

 VI. Dylan and Max fly back toward the house.

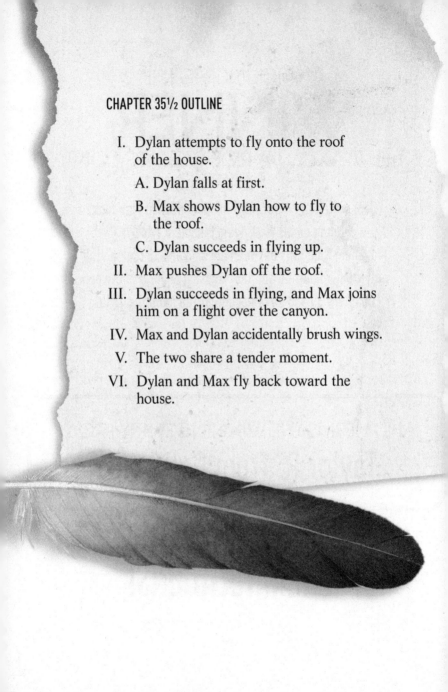

"Okay," he said somewhat confidently. I laughed to myself as he tried to get off the ground and onto the roof. This was going to be fun. His wings flapped a couple times before he crashed back to the ground for the second time that day.

"Try getting a running start. Give yourself enough room," I said, trying to be helpful without sending the wrong message. "Like this." I shook out my wings and took a couple steps backward. Running forward, I leaped off the ground and beat my wings until my shoe brushed the gutter. I landed silently on the roof and turned to Dylan.

He was staring at me, uncertainty reflected in his eyes. "Do I have to try now?"

"Um . . . duh." Apparently Dr. God had forgotten to clone common sense into Dylan's brain. Dylan took several steps back, like I had, and then ran forward. He jumped into the air and flapped his wings hard, extreme concentration showing on his face. Miraculously, he managed to raise himself up into the air and make it to the roof. As he landed, I could see his face glowing with pride.

"Yes! I did it!" Dylan did a fist pump and looked at me expectantly.

"Um . . . yeah. Good job," I praised him, lamely. "Now let's see if we can really get you moving. I'll push you off the roof, and you've just got to flap. Once you're a good distance in the air, we'll fly to the other edge of the canyon and back. Ready?"

"I don't know, I think—" I didn't get to hear the rest of his sentence because he started plummeting toward the ground as I pushed him off the edge of the roof.

"Don't forget to flap!" I yelled after him. I sat down on the roof and counted to three in my head, expecting to hear a thud as Dylan hit the ground. But apparently he had applied what I had said, and before I knew it Dylan's tall, muscular figure was silhouetted in the night sky. I gasped in awe as his chocolate brown wings flapped, keeping him aloft. It looked almost . . . majestic. I shook the thoughts out of my head, realizing what I was thinking.

I jumped off the roof and snapped out my wings, soaring up to join Dylan.

"Great job!"

"Thanks. It's getting easier."

"I told you. With a bit of practice, it will become a lot easier." Dylan and I turned toward the canyon, coasting on the evening breeze.

A gust of wind blew, pushing me toward him. I struggled against it, but the tips of our wings brushed slightly. I looked over at him. He was staring at me intently. It looked like he was photographing me with his mind. His eyes swept over every feature of my face, and I blushed and looked away.

"We should go back," I murmured. Dylan looked disappointed, but turned back toward the house. I stared after him, my mind swirling.

Is this the end of Max and Fang . . .
and the beginning of Max and Dylan?

Find out in

Trust no one . . .
not even an angel.

ANGEL

A MAXIMUM RIDE NOVEL

JAMES PATTERSON

the next thrilling chapter in the blockbuster series

by James Patterson

Turn the page for a sneak preview!

1

I KNOW HE'LL come for me. He has to come for me. Fang wouldn't let me die here.

I'd been in the cage for days. I couldn't remember eating. I couldn't remember sleeping. I was disoriented from all the tests and the needles and the acrid disinfectant smell that had permeated my entire childhood... growing up in a lab, as an experiment. And here I was again, disoriented but still capable of a blinding rage.

Fang hadn't come for me. I would have to save myself this time.

"You! Get back!" The lab assistant's wooden billy club smashed against the door of the Great Dane–sized dog crate I was being held in every time I peered out through the front. With each strike, the door's hinges sustained more damage. Right according to plan.

Steeling my nerves, I again carefully pushed my fingers out through the bars of the crate and pressed my face against it. Timing was key: if I didn't pull back fast enough, the gorilla-like lab tech could easily crush my fingers or break my nose.

"I said, *get back!*" he repeated. *Smash!* A split-second after the club hit the weakened hinges, I kicked the door with every ounce of strength I had left.

"Hey!" The lab tech's startled yell was cut short as I shot out of the crate, a rush of seriously ticked-off mutant freak, and launched a roundhouse kick to his head. I spun again, leaping onto a table to assess my adversary.

Already a piercing klaxon was splitting the air. Shouts and pounding footsteps from the hallway added to the chaos.

I grabbed on to a pipe on a low section of the ceiling, swung forward, and slammed my feet into a white-lab-coated chest. The bully sank to his knees, unable to draw breath. This was the perfect time for me to run to the end of the table, jump off, and spread my wings.

That's where the "mutant freak" part comes in.

As hands reached for my bare feet, I shot upward, flying toward a small window high in the wall, then veered off path when a familiar dark shadow suddenly loomed.

Fang!

He was on the roof outside, watching through the window. My right-wing man! I *knew* he'd come. He had my back, like a thousand times before. He would always have my back, and I would always have his. With relief, I readied myself to crash through the glass.

The room below me was now filled with shouting people. *So long, suckers,* I thought, as I aimed and got a flying start. I'd burst through quite a few windows in my fifteen-year life, and I knew it would hurt, but I also knew pain didn't matter. Escaping mattered.

Wham! My right shoulder smashed against the glass, but it didn't break. I bounced off it and dropped hard, like a brick. Time slowed. I heard the pop of a tranquilizer gun and felt a dart pinch my leg as I crashed to the ground.

Above me, Fang watched, expressionless.

In disbelief, I realized that he wasn't here to help me after all; he wasn't going to break through the window to save me. I writhed on the shiny linoleum floor, losing consciousness.

Fang didn't have my back. Not this time.

I felt like I was I falling again. Instinct made me scramble to grab on to something, anything.

My fingers latched on to a small, hard branch. As I gasped for air, my eyes popped open, and I realized I was near the top of a tall pine tree—not in a dog crate, not back at the School. The late-morning sun bathed the Arizona mountains in rosy light. It had been a nightmare. Or, rather, a daymare.

I inhaled deeply, feeling the icy claws of adrenaline still in my veins. Cold sweat tickled my forehead and back as I tried to calm down.

It had just been a bad dream. I was free. I was safe.

Except for the worst part of the dream, the one thing that had made everything else a thousand times worse, the one thing that truly terrified and paralyzed me...

Fang really *was* gone. He *didn't* have my back. Not in the dream, not now, *never again.*

Reader's Guide

Fang: A Maximum Ride Novel is not only a fun read, but it's also full of thought-provoking story elements that are ideal for discussion groups or for your own exploration. Here are some questions to get the conversation going!

1. When Dr. Gunther-Hagen proposes an alliance between himself and the flock, why does Max immediately turn him down? Do you think Max is right never to trust anyone besides her flock? Do you think the doctor really does want to help save the world?

2. Max realizes that while her flock has some great skills, like being able to hack into computers and break into buildings, they've never gone to school to get a real education. What are some things you've learned in school that would help you save the world? What kinds of things do you know that you could teach to Max and the flock?

3. According to Max, an important part of being a leader is knowing when to back off. What are some other important qualities a good leader should have? Does Max have these qualities? Does Angel have these qualities? Whom do you admire as a leader, both in the Maximum Ride books and in real life?

4. Do you think the flock does the right thing when they ask Max to step down as leader? Do Max and Fang spend too

much time thinking about themselves and not enough time thinking about the flock? Why, do you think, does the flock resent Max and Fang's relationship?

5. When Max needs to get somewhere *fast*, she can fly almost three hundred miles per hour. If you could have any superhuman power like Max's, what would you choose? Do you think Max would choose to be a normal teenager without wings if she could?

6. The Maximum Ride books are full of action, adventure, and suspense. But they also contain lots of cool facts about famous people, places, and things, such as the Rosetta stone and the first formula for gunpowder. Can you remember any other fun facts you've learned from reading *Fang* or any of the other Maximum Ride books?

7. Fang's note says he's leaving the flock because he wants to protect them, especially Max. Does Fang do the right thing by leaving? Do you think Dylan will take Fang's place?

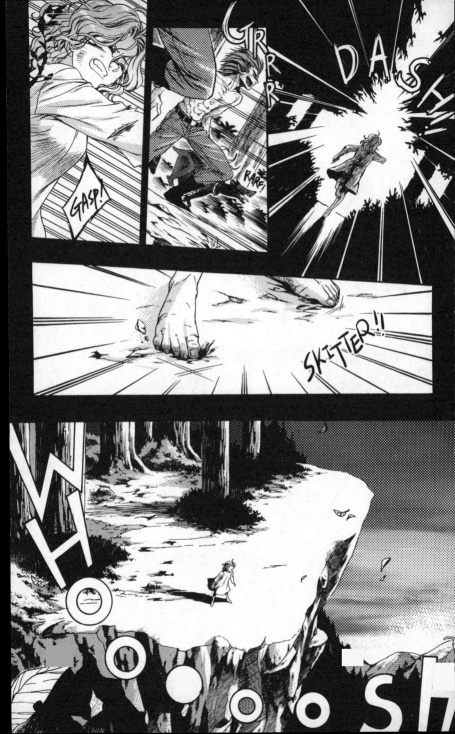

MAXIMUM RIDE

JAMES PATTERSON
& NaRae Lee

YOU WANT A FAIRY TALE, DON'T YOU?
YOU'RE NOT GOING TO FIND ONE HERE.
AND THERE IS NO HAPPILY EVER AFTER.

WITCH & WIZARD
THE FIRE

AVAILABLE NOW!

TURN THE PAGE FOR A PREVIEW!

Whit

MY LUNGS ARE bursting, and if she dies, I'll die.

We're tearing through the cramped, dank streets of the capital, running for our lives from the New Order police and their trained wolves. My calves are burning, my shoulders ache, and my mind is numb from all that's happened.

There is no more freedom. So there is no escape.

I stumble through this strange, awful world we have inherited, past a mass of the sick who are shuddering from more than just the cold. A man collapses at my feet, and I have to wrestle my arm away from a woman holding a baby and pointing at me, shrieking, "The One has judged! He has judged you!"

And then there's the blood. Mothers scratch at open pustules, and children cough into rags stained red. Half the poor in this city are dying from the Blood Plague.

And my sister is one of them.

Wisty's even paler than usual, and her slight frame is

curled over my back, her thin arms wrapped around my neck. She's in agony; her breath comes in gasps. She's murmuring about Mom and Dad, and it's ripping my heart right out of my chest.

The street pulses with waves of vacant-eyed citizens scurrying to work. A guy in a suit shoulders me to the curb, and an old man who seems to recognize me slurs something about "dark arts" under his breath and hurls a glob of spit at my cheek. Everyone has been brainwashed or brutalized into conformity. I can hear the shrieks from the abused populace as the goons hammer through them just a block behind.

They're gaining on us.

I can picture the wolves straining against their chains, foam building on their jagged teeth as they yank our pursuers forward. All missing fur and rotting flesh, they're Satan's guard dogs come to life. Something tells me that if—or when—the New Order police catch us, those animals aren't exactly going to go easy.

There's got to be an open door or a shop to slip into, but all I can see are the imposing, blaringly red banners of propaganda plastering every building. We are literally surrounded by the New Order.

Now they're right on us. The cop in the lead is a little zealot who looks like a ferret. His face is beet red under an official hat with the N.O. insignia on it. He's screaming my name and wielding a metal baton that looks like it would feel really awesome smashing across my shins.

Or through my skull.

No. I will not go out like this. *We* have the power. I think of Mom and Dad, of their faces as the smoke streaked toward them. We will avenge them. I feel a rush of rebel inspiration as lines of a banned poem thunder in my head along with the soldiers' boots.

"Rise like Lions after slumber / In unvanquishable number." I put my head down, hike up Wisty, and surge forward through the plague-ridden crowds. I won't give up.

"Shake your chains to earth like dew." I break away from the crowd, seeing an opening at the end of the street. *"Which in sleep had fallen on you— / Ye are many—they are few."* We used to be many, when the Resistance was thriving. Their faces flash before me: Janine, Emmet, Sasha, Jamilla. And Margo. Poor Margo. Our friends are long gone.

Now it's just me.

I burst through the mouth of the alley into a huge square. A mob of people gathers, looking around expectantly. Then a dozen fifty-foot-tall high-definition screens light up, surrounding us and broadcasting the latest New Order news feed. With everyone distracted, it's the perfect time to find a way out of this death trap. But I can't tear my eyes away from this particular broadcast.

It's a replay of footage from my parents' public execution.

My head swims as Mom and Dad look down from all around us, trying to be brave as they face the hateful crowd. And as I watch the people I love most in the world go up in smoke for the second time, I hear Wisty's hysterical, delirious ramblings.

"No!" She flails in my arms, trying to reach out for them just like she did that day. "Help them, Whit!" she shrieks. "We've got to help them!"

She thinks she is watching our parents' *actual execution* again.

Before I can soothe my sister, she's hacking, and I feel something hot and wet oozing down my neck and shoulders. I gag back my own bile, but the most horrific part of all is that the mess dripping down my sides is full of blood.

She hasn't got much time left.

James Patterson was selected by teens across America as the Children's Choice Book Awards Author of the Year in 2010. He is the internationally bestselling author of the highly praised Maximum Ride novels, the Witch & Wizard series, *Med Head*, *Suzanne's Diary for Nicholas*, and the detective series featuring Alex Cross and the Women's Murder Club. His books have sold more than 230 million copies worldwide, making him one of the bestselling authors of all time. He lives in Florida.